THE BREAKFAST CLUB ADVENTURES

THE BEAST BEYOND THE FENCE

This book belongs to

- - - - - - - - - - - - - - - - - - - -

Other books by Marcus Rashford

You Are a Champion:
How to Be the Best You Can Be

written with Carl Anka

Coming soon

You Can Do It:
How to Find Your Team and Make a Difference

written with Carl Anka

MACMILLAN CHILDREN'S BOOKS

MARCUS RASHFORD

Written with
Alex Falase-Koya

Illustrated
by Marta Kissi

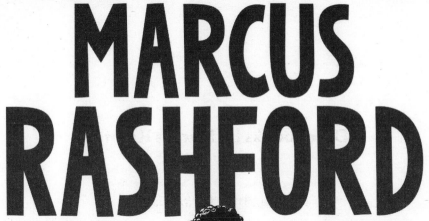

MARCUS
RASHFORD
BOOKCLUB
CHOICE

THE BREAKFAST CLUB ADVENTURES

THE BEAST BEYOND THE FENCE

Published 2022 by Macmillan Children's Books
an imprint of Pan Macmillan
The Smithson, 6 Briset Street, London EC1M 5NR
EU representative: Macmillan Publishers Ireland Ltd, 1st Floor,
The Liffey Trust Centre, 117–126 Sheriff Street Upper
Dublin 1, D01 YC43
Associated companies throughout the world
www.panmacmillan.com

ISBN 978-1-5290-7662-2

3 5 7 9 8 6 4 2

A CIP catalogue record for this book is available from the British Library.

Printed and bound by CPI Group (UK) Ltd, Croydon CR0 4YY

To every child who attends Breakfast Club,
this is your starting point.
The world is full of possibilities,
you just have to let your mind take you there.

Welcome to my Book Club.

I'm so excited to share *The Breakfast Club Adventures* with you, a book written by Alex and me especially for you. Take it home tonight and write your name in the front. It belongs to you and only you.

Jam-packed full of adventure, I hope that through this book you can broaden your horizons, you can dream bigger, you can champion and celebrate the difference in one another, and realize that difference isn't a negative, it's a strength.

How boring would life be if we were all the same?

Take the time to ask more questions. Take the time to listen and to learn about one another. When someone is low, our only answer should be to pick them back up. Remember, we all need help along the way.

Enjoy every word at your own pace and remember that there's no rush to get to the end.

Get that head of yours high and let's conquer the day together.

With love,

MR

Chapter One

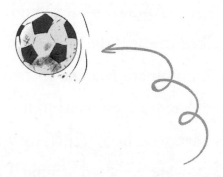

Marcus pushed open the doors to the canteen and strode into Breakfast Club. The room was bright, airy and warm, filled with the sound of kids talking loudly. The smell of *freshly made toast* and *sweet orange juice* wafted into Marcus's nose.

'Hey, Marcus!'

A large crowd was huddled around one

of the long, wooden tables that stretched through the canteen. An arm waved above everyone's heads, beckoning him over.

'Hey, Amira,' Marcus said, smiling as he walked towards the table.

'I nominate Marcus to take my turn for me,' Amira announced loudly. All eyes turned on Marcus as he **squished** through the group. They were gathered around a tall, wobbling Jenga tower on the table. He looked up at Amira with an eyebrow raised.

'Are you sure?' he asked.

Amira nodded.

'You left me one of the hardest turns,' Marcus muttered, looking at the tower. He scratched the back of his head. Then, without hesitation, he reached out and expertly tapped a piece. It slid smoothly onto the table,

leaving the rest of the tower completely intact.

An 'OOOOOOOOO' rippled through the crowd.

Marcus let out a breath of relief, feeling slightly embarrassed at all the attention. 'See you all later,' he called as he pushed through the crowd again. He walked up to the hatch to grab his food, smiling at the dinner lady as she handed him a red plastic bowl and a black plastic plate.

Turning round, he spotted his friends Oyin and Patrick sitting at the far corner of the canteen. He made his way over to them, passing more crowds of kids playing board games, doing homework, eating breakfast or just chatting to each other.

'Hey, Marcus,' Oyin and Patrick said together as he arrived.

Marcus grinned at his friends. Patrick was big, but he was faster than almost anyone else his age. His thin glasses were kept together by a piece of tape, because he had **broken** them at football practice last week. Oyin was short and had a small afro, and her feet were *magic.*

'Hey, guys,' said Marcus, taking a seat on the bench opposite them.

'What's on the menu today?' Patrick asked.

'Toast and Weetabix,' Marcus replied, grinning. 'Only the best fuel for me.' He gave a quick thumbs up.

'Yeah, on Weetabix days you're a **footballing machine** during lunch break. Almost as good as me,' Oyin said, punching him lightly on the arm.

Marcus's smile slipped slightly. He felt bad, but he was going to have to make up another excuse to get out of playing with Oyin and Patrick at lunch today. He just hadn't been able to play properly since he'd lost his ball . . .

Every time he closed his eyes he saw it happen.

He could see his left foot *Slipping* as his right foot *swung* towards the football.

He could see his toe **smashing** into the ball at the worst angle possible.

He could see the ball **whizzing up, way** over the two backpacks that made up the goal, **way** over the head of the goal-keeper, and **way** over the school fence.

And then it was gone. Lost by the building next to his school. It had happened more than a month ago, but he could still see it all.

'Hey!' Oyin poked Marcus's forehead gently. 'Is anyone home?'

Marcus blinked hard. 'What were we talking about again?' he asked.

'You were remembering kicking the ball over the fence,' Patrick said.

Marcus sighed. 'How did you know?'

'Marcus, whenever you go quiet these days you're thinking about that ball,' Oyin said.

Patrick nodded, taking off his glasses and giving them a good clean before placing them back on his face.

'I just *know* I can still get it back,' Marcus muttered.

'We walked along the whole fence, Marcus, looking through to see if we could see it,' Oyin said kindly. 'It just wasn't there.'

'Maybe I just wasn't looking hard enough,' Marcus said. 'Maybe I should have gone over.'

'Marcus, you know the rules,' Oyin said,

lowering her voice. 'We don't go over the fence if we can't see the ball. **It's too risky.**'

'Yeah, you heard Mrs Miller, right?' said Patrick. Marcus nodded, thinking about their **terrifying** head teacher. 'She's coming down hard on people. It's like getting a **red card,** but in your school life!' Patrick leaned back in his chair. 'I heard that some kid from Maths Club got detention for a month for going over that fence.'

'What's so special about the football anyway?' Oyin asked. Marcus opened his mouth to respond, but before he could speak a deep voice came from behind them.

'Ah, here we have our table of young footballers.' Marcus turned to see Mr Anderson, one of his favourite teachers, smiling at them, his blue eyes crinkling at the corners. Mr Anderson was tall and had short grey hair, and every day without fail he wore a tweed jacket with patches sewn on at the elbows. He taught music, but often ran the Breakfast Club too.

'Not just that, we also have a trumpet player,' Patrick said, referring to himself.

'And a maths person. I'm good at maths.' Oyin pointed at her chest.

'Well, I'll be sure to keep that in mind!' Mr Anderson said. 'And I hope you lot have done your homework?'

He raised an eyebrow.

'Yes, of course we have, Mr Anderson,' said Oyin quickly.

'Ah, Oyin, that's what you always say,' Mr Anderson sighed. He pretended to roll his eyes, **winked** at them and then walked off.

'Young footballers?' Marcus muttered glumly. 'Not me so much any more, not when I'm still on the bench.' Just saying that phrase felt difficult, like he was bringing something up from the back of his throat. 'I have plenty of time for homework.'

'Yeah, but everyone knows you're good enough to be a starter, you're just –' Patrick paused – 'a little off right now.' He pushed his glasses back up his nose.

Marcus looked down at the table.

'Marcus,' Oyin began tentatively, 'why don't you let us help y—'

'Thanks for offering,' Marcus interrupted before she could finish. He forced a smile onto his face. 'I do appreciate it — I really do — but I already have someone who can help me get my touch back. I just need to wait for her to come back.'

Patrick and Oyin sighed.

Marcus felt awkward under their gaze. 'I'm going to the bathroom,' he said, standing up. He knew they meant well, but they didn't understand that he didn't need their help. He just had to do what he always did when he was having a **rough patch.** Marcus had to get the help of his cousin, Lola.

He walked out of the canteen and headed down the corridor.

Everything at Rutherford Secondary School was old, from the way the doors locked to the windows that **rattled** when the wind blew violently. Even the forest that **stretched** out behind the school was ancient. But it was all really well maintained. Marcus liked feeling like a *time traveller* here. Even though this was only his first year, it felt as if it was his school.

Marcus slipped his hands into his pockets, blinking in surprise as his right hand brushed up against something. It felt like a piece of paper. He came to a stop in the corridor and pulled it out, staring at it in confusion.

Written in well-practised handwriting were the words:

 Do you want to join the BCI?

If it wasn't for the marks that the pen had pressed into the page, Marcus would have thought that the words had come out of a printer.

'The BCI . . .' Marcus frowned. He had no idea what it stood for.

He peered down the corridor, searching for the person who had slipped him the note, but the hallway was empty.

There were two square boxes drawn onto the page. **YES** was written below the one on the left, and **NO** was written below the one on the right.

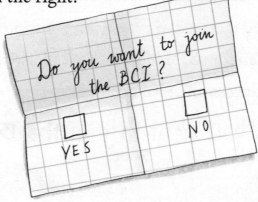

Yes or no? How was he supposed to decide if he wanted to join something he knew nothing about? Marcus's eyes flicked between the boxes uncertainly.

Suddenly there was a loud **squeak** from down the hall.

Marcus glanced up. A classroom door ahead was swinging closed, but he hadn't seen who'd gone through it. Was it whoever had slipped him this note?

He set off towards the door, his body moving before he had time to think. He was almost there when he suddenly realized what he was doing.

He stopped and smiled to himself. Why was he chasing some random person because they *might* have tried to prank him with a note? **It was all silly.**

Shaking his head, he turned round and walked back to Breakfast Club.

Chapter Two

As soon as Marcus reached their table, Oyin leaned in and said in an undertone, 'Something odd just happened.'

Marcus raised his eyebrows questioningly. He slipped his hand back into his pocket and gripped the note tight.

'The people on that table came over asking to talk to you.' Patrick pointed to a table at the far end of the canteen. Marcus looked, but he couldn't see who was sitting there as they had their back to him. All he could see was a *long, black ponytail.*

'They wouldn't tell us what it was about.' Oyin shook her head. 'Are you going to go?'

'I guess so,' Marcus said, shrugging. Although he didn't want to admit it, he was intrigued by the note.

He got to his feet and walked across the canteen to where the girl with the ponytail was sitting. 'Hi,' he said, a little nervously, once he got there. But the girl didn't respond.

Marcus felt someone move behind him and he looked round **quickly.** He relaxed when he saw a friendly face he recognized. 'Hi, Lise,' he said.

'Hi,' Lise said. 'We're glad you decided to come.'

Marcus looked at her. 'We?' he said, raising an eyebrow as she took a seat next to the girl with the ponytail. Marcus walked round the table and sat down. Lise was smiling at him, but the other girl looked serious.

It was Stacey To. **The new girl.** She had joined year seven later than the rest of them, just after the Christmas holidays. Marcus didn't know a lot about her. She mostly kept to herself, but he had seen her in the library a few times. He had never seen Lise and Stacey hanging out before, although Lise was super popular and friends with everyone, so it kind of made sense. He wondered what they wanted from him.

'You didn't answer my note,' Stacey said. She spoke in a very **low voice,** as if she was trying not to be overheard.

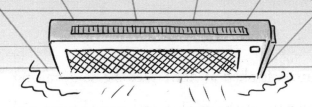

'You're the one who put it in my pocket?' Marcus asked, his suspicions confirmed. 'Why didn't you just say something?'

'Some things require a little bit of . . . **secrecy.**' She had a mysterious smile on her face. 'You'll understand later.'

'I don't know if I will,' Marcus muttered.

He was getting very **confused.**

'Do you know why we picked this table?' Stacey went on, ignoring him.

'No.'

'It's the furthest table from the one where Mr Anderson sits,' she said. 'And the air conditioner helps to drown out the voices and keep what we say private.' She pointed up at the **rumbling machine** on the ceiling above them.

'OK, so what's this got to do with the note in my pocket?' Marcus asked. 'What is the BCI?'

'So now you understand how far we're going to keep this meeting and what we're going to say a **secret,** I hope you'll do the same,' Stacey said, still not answering his questions. 'Keep this a secret, even from them.' She gestured at the table where Patrick and Oyin were sitting, pretending not to watch what they were doing.

Marcus was unconvinced.

'If you promise,' Stacey went on, 'I'll tell you all about **the BCI,** and how we can help you get your football back.'

At once, Marcus sat up straighter in his seat. 'My football?' he said, his voice growing louder in his excitement. 'You know something about my football?'

Lise hushed Marcus. *'Shhh.'*

But Marcus was desperate to hear Stacey's next words. 'What is the BCI?' he said eagerly. 'And what does it have to do with my football?'

'It will all make sense – just give us a chance to explain everything. Lise, can you please give me a hand?' Lise reached into her backpack and brought out a wide paper banner, which she smoothed onto the table.

'We,' Stacey said grandly, 'are **the Breakfast Club Investigators.**' She stood up, put her foot on the chair and pointed to the words on the banner, where they had been scrawled in big handwriting.

'The Breakfast Club Investigators . . .' Marcus said slowly. He shifted uncomfortably. Something about Stacey's absolute confidence and how confusing she was made it difficult for Marcus to get into the conversation. It was like *jumping onto a moving train.* 'What does any of this have to do with Breakfast Club?' he asked eventually.

'Well, Breakfast Club is the best time to do any investigations. School hasn't started yet, so it's just us here. **Us Breakfast Club members have the whole school to ourselves!'** Stacey said with a huge grin. Lise nodded in agreement.

'So —' Marcus looked around, trying to find something to say that would help him make sense of the conversation — 'what are you even investigating here?'

'That's a great question. What *are* we investigating?' Stacey nodded at Lise again, and this time Lise brought out a bunch of printed photos from her backpack. 'Well, in our short time here we've taken on quite a few cases,' Stacey said impressively. 'The case of the **missing** PE clothes, the case of the **rattle** underneath the English classroom and the case of the **mysterious shadow** in the school hall.'

Photos of
PE clothes,
the English
classroom and the
school hall were
now on the table.

'You actually
have cases? So
people ask you
for help?'
Marcus was
impressed.

'Well, no, not yet . . . We need to build
our name a little first,' Stacey admitted.

'The trouble is,' said Lise, 'that with the
missing PE clothes, the teacher just left the
window open and they got **blown**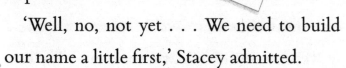
to the back of the class. The rattle underneath

the English classroom, well, that was just a **vibrating** phone that had slipped through a crack in the floor. And the mysterious shadow in the school hall – that was just a bird that had got stuck inside.'

'So, you solved all those cases?' Marcus asked.

Stacey frowned. 'Yes, but who cares? We can't build our name if we don't find something weird or unexpected. Where are all the **aliens?**

And **vampires?**

And **werewolves?**'

'Aliens and vampires?' Marcus repeated.

'I mean, I'd even settle for a mummy or a giant robot.' Stacey threw her arms up.

Marcus paused. He didn't know if she was joking or not. 'But none of those things exist,' he said.

Stacey leaped up out of her chair again. '**Yet.** They don't exist **yet.** We don't have proof **yet.**' Every time she said 'yet', Stacey poked the air.

Marcus stared at her, not really knowing what to do, but a small smile began to spread over his face.

'People once thought the Earth was flat, and that the Earth was at the centre of the solar system,' Stacey added.

'I don't know if that's the same,' said Marcus.

'**It is!** This world of ours is full of mysteries. We just have to reach out and **grab** them. Like the mystery of what happened to your football.' Marcus's heartbeat quickened. 'Now, whenever a ball goes over that school fence, it disappears. The whole time we've been at Rutherford, not one person has been able to get a ball back.'

'Think about it,' Lise added. 'Have you ever seen anyone go into or out of that building next door? Do you even know what that building is?'

Stacey gave him a piercing look. 'The construction stopped ages ago, but the building still hasn't opened.'

Marcus swallowed. His mouth was suddenly dry.

'And it's not just footballs. Toys, books, games consoles, anything that ends up there vanishes like **that.**' Stacey clicked her fingers.

'Do you think you can find my football?' Marcus said, trying not to sound too hopeful.

'Yes,' Stacey said, without missing a beat.

Marcus cleared his throat, thinking hard. 'But why are you interested in it? You wanted to find aliens and vampires, and now you're looking for footballs.'

'Because you've lost something important to you, and every detective in the Breakfast Club Investigators can relate to that.' Stacey scrunched up her fist and thumped it onto her leg.

'Now that deserves an investigation!'

Marcus's head was spinning. He nodded a couple of times, then he finally spoke.

'I'm sorry, but it's a no,' he said. 'I'm not joining you.'

Chapter Three

Marcus found it difficult to focus that day. His attention kept *drifting* off to his football. He wanted to believe that Stacey and Lise could help him, but he just couldn't see how joining some random group could get his ball back. A group led by someone who believed in **vampires** and **zombies,** but that was supposed to be able to investigate real-life mysteries . . . None of it made sense to Marcus.

By the time the bell rang for the end of the day, Marcus was exhausted. He slowly trudged the path back to his flat, his mind still reeling. The spring air was mild as he walked, and he noticed that the leaves were starting to grow back on the trees.

As soon as he had reached his estate, he heard the unmistakable sounds of kids playing football down at the **Cage.** It was like a never-ending game in there – there was always someone kicking or throwing a ball around. Tall sheets of metal mesh fencing towered over the space, which the kids used for all types of sports.

'Hey, Marcus, wanna play?' shouted Tunde. He lived just a few doors down from Marcus.

'Nah, not today,' Marcus called back.

'Maybe tomorrow.' He felt a pang of guilt at the lie; he knew that his answer would be the same tomorrow.

Tunde walked over to the Cage fence. 'You've said that about a thousand times now. You haven't played in, like, **a month!** Are you not

interested in football any more?'

Marcus looked up sharply. 'Of course I'm interested,' he shot back. Then he took a breath and smiled. 'Sorry, Tunde, I just have this back injury that isn't going away.

As soon as that's sorted, I'll be back on the pitch.' He felt bad for lying, but he just didn't want Tunde to see him like this, **with his touch this bad.** He needed to wait for Lola to show him how to get better.

'OK, we'll play together soon, Marcus!' Tunde waved him off and went back to the game of football.

Marcus went slowly up the concrete stairs and followed the hallway down to number 305. He unlocked the door and stepped onto the brown carpet of the hallway, leaning on the worn white wallpaper as he took off his shoes. His mum must have finished early at the hospital, because he could hear her in the kitchen making dinner.

'Hi, Marcus,' she called.

'Hi, Mum,' Marcus said, walking into the

kitchen and giving her a quick hug. He slung his backpack under the dining table then took a seat.

Their kitchen was a small space that was used expertly. Pans hung from hooks on the walls, and tonnes of spices sat in containers on shelves. Some people might have called the flat small, but to Marcus it was cosy. **It was home.**

'So, how was your day?' his mum asked.

'It was . . .' Marcus hesitated. 'All right.'

His mum raised her eyebrows. 'Just all right?'

'Well . . .' Marcus said.

'Well?' his mum prompted.

'Well, I think I was asked to join a **secret society,**' Marcus admitted. He'd been holding it in all day, and suddenly he realized how much he wanted to discuss what had happened at Breakfast Club.

His mum stopped stirring the pot in front of her and turned round to look at him. 'OK,' she said slowly. 'A secret society?'

'Yeah,' Marcus said. 'It's run by this girl called Stacey who believes in ghosts and vampires.' Marcus relayed the whole conversation he'd had with Lise and Stacey as he laid the table. Their cases, how they **lured** him in by saying they knew how to get his football and how they'd *sworn him to silence.* His mum laughed in all the right places. She was always the person to whom he could tell anything and everything. She knew how important the football was to him, but she just let him talk, without telling him what to do, and Marcus loved her for that.

After dinner, Marcus and his mum watched

some TV together, and then he went off to his bedroom to do his homework. Just before bed, he heard his mum call out.

'**Marcus!** You've got a phone call!'

Marcus knew who it would be. 'Do I have to, Mum?' he called back.

'You haven't spoken to her in weeks.' Marcus's bedroom door opened. His mum was standing in the doorway, one hand on her hip and the other holding her phone to her chest to muffle the microphone. 'Get on the phone.' Her tone made it clear that it wasn't a request.

Marcus **groaned** under his breath, then walked over and took the phone from his mum. The voice on the other side was scratchy and static-filled, but it was unmistakable.

'Hey, Marcus,' Lola said.

'Hey,' Marcus replied. He tapped his foot.

'So, how've you been doing over there?' Marcus hoped she wouldn't ask him how

practice was going. He didn't want to talk about losing his touch, not over the phone, and especially not without the football.

'I've been good,' Lola replied in a chirpy tone. 'I'm going to be back on Sunday.'

'Sure,' Marcus said absently. He stopped speaking, suddenly realizing what she'd said. **'Wait!** Did you say you'd be back on Sunday? As in – **six days' time?'**

'What days' time?' Lola's voice came through even more crackly than before. 'Sorry, Marcus, the connection's really bad. I'll have to call you back.'

'Oh – don't worry,' Marcus said quickly, trying to sound happy. 'I'll see you soon, OK?'

'See y—' The phone went dead, and Marcus handed it back to his mum.

Less than a week. How was he supposed to find that football in that time? He had spent the last month trying to find the football and had got nowhere, and now he was supposed to do it in less than a *week?* Six days!

Marcus bit his lip. Lola had given that ball to him when she'd gone off to America. She'd told him to take care of it until she got back – and if he didn't have it when she got back then he worried that there was no way that she'd help him get his touch back.

He knew what he had to do.

Chapter Four

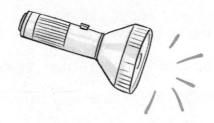

The next day, when Marcus got to Breakfast Club, he nodded at Patrick and Oyin but he didn't sit next to them. Ignoring their confused faces, he went all the way over to the back of the canteen where Lise and Stacey were sitting.

'I want to join,' Marcus announced.

Stacey looked up at him in excitement. **'Excellent!** What changed your mind?'

'It doesn't matter,' Marcus said. 'You still think you'll be able to find the football, right?'

'I'm sure we can,' Stacey replied with a grin.

'Great to have you on board, Marcus,' said Lise, beaming. She turned to Stacey, eyes bright. 'So, Stace, what's the plan?'

Stacey rubbed her hands together in glee, as if she had been waiting for this question. 'Investigators,' she said loftily, 'there's only one thing to do. We'll have to go next door, into that **mysterious building,** and see what clues we can uncover.'

Marcus hesitated. He hadn't been expecting that. He exchanged a nervous glance with Lise.

'We'll have to do it before Breakfast Club even starts,' Stacey went on, 'so that the teachers don't catch us. That's the only way we can get the football back.' Stacey caught Marcus's eye.

Marcus rubbed his chin, thinking. He wasn't sure they should be going through the fence, but he didn't have any other option to get his football back in time for Lola's return. 'I guess you're right,' he said eventually. 'But we have to make sure **nobody sees us,** or we'll be in big trouble.'

'Great. It's settled, then. Tomorrow we sneak through the fence before Breakfast Club gets started. Agreed? We'll need to come in twenty minutes before Breakfast Club even starts,' Stacey said. 'And, if you can bring any supplies that might help in our investigation, please do.'

Marcus spent all day trying to figure out what he could bring for their investigation.

But by the time the last bell of the day had rung he still hadn't had any ideas. Marcus joined the mob of kids rushing through the halls and bumped into Patrick and Oyin outside.

'You wanna play?' Patrick asked, bouncing a football. Marcus smiled, realizing that they had waited for him to arrive.

'Well, I would, but – you know.' Marcus didn't have to say the words, but they understood. **His touch.**

'Who cares? It's just us,' Oyin said as she circled behind Marcus and began to push him forward.

'Come on. *Please!*' Patrick said.

'OK, OK,' Marcus said finally, giving them a reluctant grin. He'd have to search for something to bring to the investigation later that evening – he only hoped his mum had a late shift, so she wouldn't ask what he was doing.

They made their way to the nearby park and stood a couple of metres apart, passing the ball between them.

'I'm Vivianne Miedema!' Oyin said as she swung a boot at the football. It soared to Patrick.

'I'm Robin van Persie!' Patrick said, thumping the football over to Marcus.

'I'm –' Marcus started as he pulled back his leg, but the moment his foot hit the ball, he stopped. It skidded off between where Patrick and Oyin stood – **'just Marcus,'** he muttered.

'It doesn't matter, Marcus,' Patrick said after he'd got the ball back. 'Anyway, how come you didn't sit with us at Breakfast Club this morning? You sat with your new friends, Stacey and Lise, instead.'

Marcus felt his cheeks grow hot. 'I don't have any new friends! You guys are my friends.'

'Patrick's just teasing,' Oyin said. 'It's good to have new friends! Patrick's been hanging out with the Music Club recently. He met some of them after his *trumpet* lesson.'

'Some of them come to Breakfast Club too! And you, you have the **Maths Club** people you've been talking to,' Patrick said.

'They're super smart, and really fun.' Oyin grinned. 'So, what's the deal with your new friends?'

'They're just . . . helping me with something. They think they can get my football back,' Marcus said hesitantly.

'Well, is it going well?' Patrick asked. Then his face darkened. 'You lot aren't thinking of going **over the fence** to look for it, are you?'

'Of course not,' said Marcus quickly. He felt bad for lying, but he didn't want them to worry. They just didn't understand how much that football meant to him.

And, if he was being honest with himself, a tiny part of him was worried that they might just be able to talk him out of **investigating** further.

★

When Marcus got home later that evening, the flat was empty. He breathed a sigh of relief. His mum wasn't home yet. She probably had a late shift, which worked for him, as he could look for supplies without her getting **suspicious.**

Marcus searched **high** and **low** for something that might come in handy, from the drawer in the kitchen filled with *junk* that never got used, to the space in between the couch cushions. He checked under the wardrobe and in all the cupboards, riffling through everything.

Thirty minutes later, he was **sweating** in his tracksuit. He hadn't found anything at all that might be useful. The closest thing had been a paper clip and some Blu Tack. Exhausted, Marcus went back to his room and **belly flopped** onto his bed. His arms hung down either side of it, slowly swinging back and forth.

And then his hand hit something. Something rubbery, under his bed.

He leaned over and picked it up. His eyes went wide, and he pumped his fist. It was a hand-held torch.

He fiddled with the torch, twisting it back and forth, but nothing happened.

Marcus *slowly unscrewed* its bottom and peered inside, clicking his tongue up against the top of his mouth when he saw the problem. It had no batteries in it.

He got to his feet and looked out of the window. The sun had begun to set. His mum had always warned him about going outside after dark, but this was an **emergency.** He ran into the kitchen and took a look at the clock. It was seven, which meant that he would have fifteen, maybe twenty minutes **max** before his mum got home.

Marcus threw on his trainers and a coat and sped out of the door, tearing down the stairs of the estate. He ran all the way to the corner shop.

The door **beeped** as Marcus flung himself inside, breathing heavily.

The man at the counter was watching a small TV that hung from the ceiling, which was playing a programme in a language Marcus couldn't understand. 'Hey, Marcus,' the shopkeeper said in his gravelly voice, glancing at him.

'Hi, Mr Diallo,' Marcus replied when he had regained his breath.

'How's your mum?' Mr Diallo asked.

'She's fine, thanks,' Marcus said as he walked around. 'How are your family?' He chatted to the shopkeeper as he searched shelf after shelf as quickly as he could, until he finally found what he was looking for.

He took the batteries up to the counter.

'That'll be four pounds fifty,' Mr Diallo

said, without taking his eyes off the TV.

Marcus's heart **sank.** He hadn't checked the price beforehand.

He reached into his pocket and took out everything that was in there. He counted out a fifty pence coin, a twenty pence coin, a button and a **piece of fluff** on the counter. He closed his eyes in frustration. What was he supposed to do now?

Mr Diallo looked down from his show and chuckled, **pushing** the contents of Marcus's pockets back across the counter towards him.

'You don't have enough money for that,' he said.

'I know,' said Marcus dejectedly. 'I'll put them back.'

'Hang on a second.' Mr Diallo reached

beneath the counter and pulled out the remote control for the TV overhead. He took out the batteries. 'I only started using these a couple of days ago. They should work fine for you.'

Marcus looked at him in surprise. 'But – but what about your TV?'

'I have a thousand batteries in this shop – I'll be fine. Now, do you want these or not?' Mr Diallo asked gruffly.

'I do! Thank you so much, Mr Diallo!' Marcus bowed and then rushed out of the store, hardly daring to believe his luck. His community had the best people!

Back in his room, Marcus picked up the torch once again and fitted the batteries. In an instant, a **bright beam** of light shot up at his face.

'**Yes!**' Marcus exclaimed. Then he laughed at his own reaction. Since when was he so excited to go adventuring with this group? It must be because he wanted to get his ball back. That was all it was.

Chapter Five

Marcus woke up to the sound of his alarm clock. He **slapped** at it until it fell silent, wondering why it was way earlier than when he usually woke up. Then he remembered.

Today, they were going over the fence. He and the Breakfast Club Investigators.

All the excitement he had from last night was now **weighed down** by a new feeling of **dread** in the pit of his stomach. Now that it was so close, he couldn't help thinking about what would happen if they were caught. Or if something went wrong. This morning, he would be relying on a group of people that he barely knew. A group that he'd only joined as his last resort. Thinking about it made his throat dry.

For a moment he just lay there, debating whether to just not go, but a single thought got him moving. He only had four days left to get that football back.

The clock was ticking.

Marcus got dressed and pulled on a hoodie over his shirt. He didn't know what might happen this morning, and he didn't want his mum to get suspicious if he came home with dirty school uniform.

It was foggy outside, and it took Marcus longer than usual to walk to school. He almost didn't see Stacey until she was right in front of him.

'Are you ready?' she said.

Marcus closed his eyes, blotting out everything except an image of the football in his mind. 'Yeah, I think I am,' he said.

'Good.' Stacey was grinning widely, her excitement shining clearly on her face.

As soon as Lise arrived, Marcus said, 'Let's go,' to the two of them. But they just stood still.

'We're still waiting on one more person,' Stacey said.

As if on cue, a figure *strode out* of the mist. 'Hey, guys,' it said.

Marcus stared at Asim Choudhry in

surprise. Asim was a boy in his class, but Marcus had never really spoken to him properly before. Not because Marcus didn't want to, it was just that Asim liked to keep to himself. He was a brilliant painter, but the problem was that he only really seemed interested in art. Marcus was surprised that he wanted to be a part of the Breakfast Club Investigators.

'All right, crew, it's time to get investigating,' Stacey said, interrupting Marcus's thoughts. 'We only have twenty minutes to get in and out.' She rubbed her hands together.

'So where do we start?' Lise asked.

Stacey looked round at them all. 'Well, first, what supplies did you all bring?'

The group huddled together in the **foggy** playground and pulled out their items from their pockets.

'A torch, good. A piece of paper?' Stacey said, pointing at the paper that Asim was holding.

'I have a pencil as well,' Asim said. 'I need it so I can draw whatever we run into.'

'OK, sure.' Stacey shrugged. 'And – a ball of **rubber bands?**' She was looking at Lise's item, clearly unimpressed.

'My mam always says you never know when you're going to need a rubber band,' Lise said cheerfully.

'OK, top marks for Marcus, low marks for everyone else.' Stacey gave a stern **thumbs down** to Lise and Asim.

'What about you?' Marcus said, pointing squarely at Stacey. She was the leader here, after all.

'Oh, well, I kinda completely forgot.' When Marcus frowned, she continued, 'I was thinking of what would happen if it was a giant robot taking all the stuff, and I started thinking about how we would beat it and that took a long, long while. So I don't have any physical supplies, but if we run into a **ɡiant robot** I've got a tonne of ideas.' She finished with a wide grin.

'I don't know if that's very useful to us right now.' Marcus shook his head and checked his battered old watch. 'Um, shouldn't we hurry? We now only have fifteen minutes to get in and out of there.'

Stacey nodded her agreement and led them across the playground towards a small gap in the school's fence. Unbidden, the stern voice of their head teacher came into Marcus's mind.

'The fence will be fixed soon. Do not under any circumstances go through the fence.'

'Marcus, come *on*.' Stacey's voice suddenly sounded really far away.

Marcus's head whipped round, but he couldn't see anyone. The fog was beginning to clear up, but he still couldn't see through to the other side of the fence. The others must have gone through already.

'**Marcus!**' A warbling voice called his name again.

He let out a deep breath, bent down and crawled under the break in the fence.

He straightened up to find himself in between Lise and Asim. The group stood

in a thin alleyway, with the school fence on
one side and the tall, grey building in front

of them. It only had a few windows, and its **concrete walls** didn't tell them anything about what might be inside.

It hadn't always been here. Marcus remembered the space being empty and overrun with weeds once upon a time, back when he was in primary school. Then, a couple of years ago, people started building here, but still nothing had opened.

Marcus had a quick look up and down the alleyway on the off chance that he might see his football, but it was nowhere to be found.

'Come **on,** Marcus. You didn't think it was going to be that easy, did you?' Stacey patted Marcus on the shoulder as she walked past him, towards the back of the grey building. He scowled at her as she passed.

The fog kept them from seeing beyond the fence under which they had slipped. It seemed as if they had been cut off from the school, as if they were in another world completely.

It was eerie.

Marcus swallowed his fear and kept trudging after Stacey and Asim. He couldn't turn back now. He kept his eyes on Asim's paint-stained backpack ahead of him as he walked next to Lise.

'Hey,' Marcus whispered, leaning in close to Lise, 'how did you get Asim to join, anyway?'

'Oh, well, we didn't *get* him to join,' Lise whispered back. 'He just walked over one day and asked to join, so we said yes.'

Marcus frowned as a wisp of fog *curled*

past his left foot. He flinched at the movement, swallowed then kept walking forward.

'Just like that, out of the blue?' Marcus said to Lise.

'Yep, just like that.' Lise shrugged.

'And you don't wonder why he joined?' Marcus pressed. It wasn't like he was suspicious of Asim or anything, but he was curious.

'We all have things we're trying to find, Marcus. That's why you joined, right?' Lise shivered, and glanced over her shoulder.

'Yeah, that's true,' he admitted. 'What about you and Stacey, though? What are you trying to find?'

'I haven't lost anything. I'm not here for that, but Stacey is looking for something. I don't know what it is, but I know it's important to her,' Lise murmured.

Marcus was silent as he considered this. He wondered why Asim and Stacey didn't want to tell anyone what they were looking for.

Eventually, the group reached the end of the building, where a sea of grey cement extended onwards as far as the eye could see. It had odd painted markings on it.

What are they? A sign for incoming aliens?

Marcus thought wildly.

'That's a **huge** car park,' Lise said in a hushed voice.

Marcus breathed a sigh of relief. Then he laughed softly under his breath. He couldn't believe he had been so freaked out. Stacey's crazy theories about monsters were clearly getting under his skin.

Stacey pointed to a large steel door at the back of the building, which had a code panel next to it. It was the first door they'd come across. 'We have to go in,' she said decisively.

'Do we really?' Asim asked. Marcus glanced at him; he looked terrified.

'That's the way forward. *I can feel it,*' Stacey said. Her eyes had an intense look in them. 'I've got this.' She walked over to the door and pulled it as hard as she could, but it didn't budge. 'OK, I don't got this. Lise, you're into technology – don't you have some sort of cool tech way to hack this door?' She looked up at the code panel.

'Unfortunately, no,' Lise said with an apologetic smile.

'She's not a magician,' Marcus added.

'I'm just checking. Technology can be

like *magic* sometimes.' Stacey flashed Lise a grin.

'That door's locked. There's no way in.' Asim picked at the paint stains on his knees. 'We have to go back to school. We've got less than ten minutes left.'

Marcus glanced at his watch again. Asim was right. They probably should turn back, but Marcus knew that they might never have another chance at this. Or at least not before Lola came home. If they were going to find the football here, they'd have to do it **now.**

'This window's open,' Marcus said, walking over to a window further along the wall. 'I can boost someone up, but they won't have much of a view of what's inside before they go through.'

'I'll do it,' Stacey said without even a moment's hesitation. Marcus stood underneath the window with his back against the wall, bracing himself. Stacey walked over, then placed her foot on his interlinked fingers. With a great **heave,** Marcus pushed her up. She scrambled for a moment and then dropped in with a **crash.**

Marcus took two steps back, glancing in panic at Asim and Lise.

The three of them stood there, frozen.

'Stace?' Lise called out uncertainly. There was no reply.

Then the locked door eased open. Stacey did a smart curtsey in the doorway. 'Were you guys worried?' she asked.

Lise breathed a sigh of relief. 'Of course,' she replied.

'Kinda, yeah,' Asim said.

Marcus didn't say anything, his heart still recovering from its overactivity.

The gang walked through the door into **pitch-black.** The only light came from the open doorway, which quickly disappeared as they moved deeper into the room. Marcus's heart began to pound again as he took slow,

heavy steps forward. He slipped his hand
into his pocket and took out his torch. Its
beam of light fell onto large cardboard

boxes all around them, wrapped up tight in plastic.

The group was completely silent. Dust tickled Marcus's nose. He was desperate to sneeze, but was terrified of making a noise. The air felt heavy with tension. What if there was something here,

lurking in the darkness?

The beam of Marcus's torch fell across a doorway up ahead. Without talking, Marcus, Stacey, Asim and Lise all crept towards it. Stacey pushed the door gingerly. It creaked open, but they couldn't make out what was in the next room. Asim felt around on the wall and found a light switch. When he turned it on, they all yelped; the light was so bright that they couldn't see.

Then their eyes adjusted.

'Is this . . . ?' Lise trailed off.

'Yeah. It is,' Stacey replied.

A supermarket. But it wasn't like any supermarket Marcus had seen before. The shelves were bare, there was no hum from the fridges and freezers, and the cash registers were nowhere to be seen. It was completely empty.

Chapter Six

The silence felt crushing.

There was something wrong about this place.

Marcus could feel it, but he couldn't quite put his finger on what it was. Alert, he walked slowly around the shop, looking for any sign of his football.

'What's this?' Lise suddenly called out.

Her voice echoed around the empty room.

Marcus walked out of the end of the aisle to see Lise and Asim crouching down. Asim was staring intently at something on the floor in front of them, and his hands were holding his piece of paper and pencil. The pencil flitted up and down, sketching.

Marcus and Stacey joined them, and they all peered down at a small mound of broken plastic, ripped up wires and a cracked screen on the ground. A thick liquid coated the entire thing. It looked almost like **snot** to Marcus.

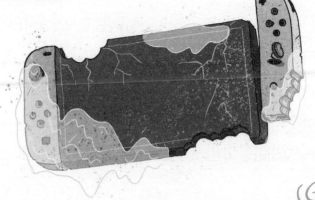

'I don't know what it is, but it's really wet and sticky,' Asim said with a **disgusted** look on his face.

Marcus squinted at it. 'It's a Nintendo Switch,' he said.

'A Nintendo Switch?' Asim looked up, his eyes wide with confusion.

'It's a games console that you can carry around with you. One of my friends has one,' Marcus said. Marcus didn't include the fact that he had been obsessed with getting one himself, but he knew that his family could never afford something like it.

'I know what a Switch is, but what's it doing in here?' said Asim.

'And why does it look all **chewed up** and broken?' Lise added, reaching out towards the Switch, but Asim's pencil swooped down and slapped her hand away.

'Don't touch it – I'm still drawing,' Asim said, annoyed.

Marcus frowned. He, Stacey and Lise stared at Asim until he eventually straightened up. 'OK, I'm done now,' he said.

'What is that **slime** all over it? I've never seen something like that before,' Marcus asked.

'That's **ectoplasm,** Marcus,' Stacey said, as though it was obvious.

'Ectoplasm?' Marcus, Asim and Lise said all at once.

'Goo left behind by **ghosts** or other supernatural beings. Evidence that they were here. I read about it in a book.' Stacey's eyes were bright in the fluorescent lighting.

'Makes sense,' Lise replied, pushing up her glasses.

'Does it?' Asim asked, looking sceptical. 'I haven't heard of that before.'

'Yeah, are you sure?' Marcus added.

Marcus and Asim caught each other's eyes.

'Yes, one hundred and ten per cent. **It's real ectoplasm!**' Stacey replied. 'We need to take it all with us. I'm sure it has some clues!'

'We can wrap it up with one of the pieces of paper Asim brought,' Marcus suggested.

Asim's face darkened. It looked like he was going to protest, then he caught himself. 'All right,' he said. He carefully scooped up the broken Nintendo Switch with his paper, then put it into his bag.

And then, as soon as the games console was out of sight, things changed.

A **deep, terrifying, howl** split the
air, sending **shivers** up Marcus's spine.
Everyone froze, slowly turning their heads to
see an impossibly **large**, shadowy figure
looming at the other end of the aisle. It was
crouched on four legs, staring at them with

a **hungry look** in its beady black eyes. Marcus's heart started hammering against his ribcage, harder than before. Every instinct he had was telling him to run, but his legs wouldn't move.

The thing took a step forward.

Marcus's jaw hung open. He couldn't close it. He—

'**Run!**' Lise screamed. Her yell broke Marcus out of whatever spell he had been under, and he turned and ran towards the exit.

Lise, Stacey and Asim were running alongside him, tearing down the aisles as fast as they could. And when Stacey and Asim fell behind, Lise grabbed both of their hands and practically *dragged* them towards the open door that led to the car park.

Another **hooooooowwwwwwwwIIIIIIIII**

ripped through the air behind them. The steady thump of clawed feet was getting closer and closer. Marcus threw himself forward, out of the supermarket and into the dark storage room. The boxes around him were practically a blur, and their feet were kicking up dust from the floor, half blinding him.

They **burst** through the open door,

back into the fog, and Marcus heaved it shut behind them as quickly as he could. They heard a **blood-curdling howl** come from inside the building, and they didn't stop running. They kept going, feet pounding and skidding across the gravel. The building loomed over them, threateningly, as they ran as fast as they could towards the hole in the fence. They threw themselves through it and only then, when they were back in the school playground, did they stop.

They all collapsed onto the ground, breathing heavily. Marcus's hands shook and his face was drenched in sweat. They lay like that for a while, too shocked by what had happened to speak.

Eventually, Stacey struggled up to her feet and began to walk round in a circle.

'**Was that a dog?** Maybe it was just a dog,' Marcus croaked.

'A dog? Have you ever seen a dog that looked like that? It was **huge,**' Stacey practically shouted. Marcus couldn't tell if she was excited or terrified.

He glanced over at Asim, who seemed to be in a daze, staring blankly up at the sky.

Lise groaned. 'And that thing didn't have any fur.' She covered her eyes with her hands.

'No fur,' Marcus repeated. His brain

started to kick into gear. Lise was right. Marcus remembered the way its skin looked, how it had seemed to somehow **pulse** and **vibrate.** Dogs don't pulse.

'Let's go back to school,' Stacey said breathlessly as the other three got to their feet. 'We'll figure it all out later.'

A loud clearing of a throat made the group spin round. Standing in front of them was a tall woman with short, greying hair and a thin, angular face. Her jaw was clenched.

It was their head teacher, Mrs Miller.

'My office. Now.' She pointed at them, then over her shoulder at the school building behind her.

Without even waiting for a response, she turned and marched off.

Chapter Seven

As Marcus walked dejectedly after Mrs Miller, all he could think about was what his mum was going to think. *What would he tell her?* Marcus got into so much trouble whenever he got his rare detentions, but even worse than his mum being cross was the disappointed look on her face.

Mrs Miller held open the door to her office as the Breakfast Club Investigators filed through. She sat behind her desk, where there were tall stacks of paper neatly piled. For a long moment, she didn't say anything. She just stared at each of them in turn.

Eventually, she spoke. 'Do you know how I saw you?'

Nobody said anything.

'My window. I saw you come out of that building,' she said. Marcus looked up. Even with all the fog, the window had a clear view of the gap in the fence. She would have been able to watch them **the whole way,** running out of the building and back through the fence.

'Should have checked before,' Stacey whispered to herself.

Lise stepped forward, her blonde hair swishing around her face. 'Mrs Miller, we're

so sorry. This was all my plan,' she said.

'No,' Stacey said firmly. 'It was me. I convinced them all to come with me. I should be punished, not them.'

Marcus looked at Stacey and Lise in wonder. He couldn't believe they were willing to take the blame.

'Oh, I know,' Mrs Miller said, looking sternly at Stacey. 'Only you could come up with something as crazy as this, Stacey To. But still, Marcus, Lise and Asim all went too. Going through the fence is one thing, but sneaking into the building itself? What would have happened if you got caught by the people who own it? **Or if you got hurt?** Do you understand how dangerous what you just did was?'

Instead of answering her questions, the Breakfast Club Investigators all spoke at once.

'Are you going to give us detention?' Lise asked with her shoulders hunched.

'Phone home?' Marcus said, biting his lip.

'Expel us from the school?' Asim said in a shaky voice.

Mrs Miller paused, and then leaned back in her chair. Her eyes scanned across the group. 'No, I'm going to do something **much worse** than that. I'm going to attack the root of the problem.' Mrs Miller clasped her hands below her chin. 'If I hear one more thing about the Breakfast Club Investigators, if you take one more step out of line, I will **ban** the group from this school. There will be no more investigating of any sort. Do you understand?' she said sharply. Then she sighed and leaned forward in her chair. 'There are other ways to have fun, you know? Club recruitment day is this Friday – I expect to see you all there, making an effort with other clubs.'

'Yes, ma'am,' Marcus, Lise and Asim said without hesitation. Marcus had no doubt that she was **completely serious.**

Only one voice was missing. Stacey was standing with her arms straight by her sides, an unreadable expression on her face.

'I said, do you understand?' Mrs Miller repeated.

Marcus elbowed her.

'Yes, ma'am,' Stacey finally sighed.

'Good. I recommend you find another club to join or take up a new hobby, because if you continue in the same way after this conversation I will not hold back in any way.' She picked up a pen from her desk. 'You're dismissed.'

The crew huddled together out of the office. Marcus checked his watch; there was still half an hour before first class.

His legs felt wobbly. When Marcus was

younger, he used to hang **upside down** on climbing frames. He and his friends would compete to see who could stay upside down for the longest amount of time, and when Marcus got off the feeling was always the same: **dizzy** and **light-headed**. That was how he felt now.

'We got off pretty lightly,' Lise said, puffing out a big breath.

Marcus began to shake his head, but that motion made him feel even dizzier. 'No, we didn't,' he said. **'It's over!** We can't investigate any more. How are we going to find the things we lost? How am I going to find my football?'

'It's not over,' Stacey muttered. She absent-mindedly chewed the edge of her thumbnail.

'What are you talking about? You heard

what she said.' Marcus jerked his head back towards Mrs Miller's office.

'It's not over,' Stacey repeated. There was fire in her brown eyes. 'All it means is that we can't get caught next time.'

Marcus cocked his head sideways. Was she saying what he thought she was saying?

'Do you really want to give up? Just like that?' Stacey asked fiercely.

'Stace, Mrs Miller did just lay down a **pretty big threat.** She's going to ban the club if we get caught again,' Lise said quietly.

'Yeah, it'd be crazy to continue,' Asim added. He picked at a lump of dried paint on his trousers.

'So what?' Stacey didn't back down. Despite her height it felt as if she was taller than all of them. 'You know what, I understand if you don't want to continue. That's totally fine. You can leave now. But me, I'm staying and seeing this through to the end.'

Stacey didn't wait for their answer. She turned on her heel and walked off to Breakfast Club.

Lise turned to look at Marcus and Asim. 'Stace is in. So . . . I guess **I'm in,**' she said with a rueful smile.

There was a long pause. Then Marcus said, 'This is the only way. I can't quit.'

'Well, I guess I'm in too, then,' Asim sighed.

The three of them followed Stacey to the canteen to catch the last half an hour of Breakfast Club before school started.

Chapter Eight

The BCI tried to avoid each other for the rest of Wednesday, not wanting to attract the attention of Mrs Miller or any other teachers. Marcus hadn't confessed to his mum about the incident when he got home, but had felt guilty about hiding it all evening, and anxious that she would somehow just **know** something had happened.

Marcus still felt tense on Thursday morning

at Breakfast Club, still **extremely shaken** by what happened in the building next door. He glanced over at Oyin and Patrick, who were in a group playing Connect Four and eating toast, and a part of Marcus wished he could be with them. But he now only had three days to get his football back.

He took a deep breath. 'OK, so what next? We went under the fence, but what did we find? **We came back with more questions** rather than any answers – or a football.' Marcus glanced over at Stacey. There was a glazed look in her eyes. 'I mean, what *was* that creature?'

'When I got home, I drew it,' Asim said, reaching into his backpack and pulling out a piece of paper.

Stacey, Marcus and Lise leaned in. It was

only a sketch, but Marcus had to admit that it looked a lot like the creature they had seen. Asim had captured details Marcus had forgotten since he had seen it in the supermarket. Its large, **gaping** mouth. Its dark, **glistening body.** Its tiny, beady eyes. Its **thick, tree-trunk-like** legs.

Marcus glanced over at Stacey again. This was around the time that she would normally call it something like a **werewolf,** but she was unusually quiet.

'What was it doing at the supermarket?' Lise asked, looking around at them all.

They were all quiet for a moment.

'I think I get it,' Marcus said slowly, leaning back in his chair. 'Why does anyone go to the supermarket . . . ? I think **it needs food.** Maybe there was some in the storage room. And that must be how the Nintendo Switch got there – it must have been damaged and left by that creature.' Marcus said all this confidently, but he couldn't help thinking that he was missing something.

'Was it trying to eat it?' Asim said, frowning.

'No, it couldn't be – or, I don't know, maybe it was!' Marcus threw up his hands, at a loss. 'Stacey, what do you think?'

Stacey was quiet for a moment. Then she suddenly said, **'We need a hideout.'**

Lise, Asim and Marcus all stared at her.

'What do you mean, we need a hideout?' Asim asked.

'Because of Mrs Miller, right?' Lise said with a worried look on her face.

'Yes, of course,' Stacey said, nodding so hard that her ponytail bounced up and down. 'If we're going to keep investigating, we need a place away from teachers' eyes. Somewhere we don't have to whisper and hide underneath an air conditioner.' She glared at the machine over their heads. 'Somewhere we can investigate things that we don't want everyone to see. If we don't have a hideout, I don't know if we can finish this case.' Stacey finished her speech with a sigh.

'Getting a hideout isn't an easy thing – you know that, right?' Asim said.

'Asim, Marcus is right about everything he just said. But what do we do now?' she asked frustratedly.

Marcus was right? That was news to him.

'I don't know,' Asim admitted.

'Same. We can't investigate this as we are right now. We **need** a hideout.' Stacey stood up.

'So, how do we get one?' Marcus asked.

'Look around at this group. What do you see?' That *manic gleam* was back in Stacey's eyes.

Marcus turned and met Asim's gaze – they

both wore the same confused look on their faces.

'People?' said Lise.

'Aaannnd?' Stacey leaned in close. 'Information. I see information. We're a group of kids who belong to a whole bunch of different clubs and groups. There's more than enough information between us to get a lead on our potential new hideout. We just have to think.'

The group fell silent. With every passing second, the weight of the silence grew, while Stacey looked at them all expectantly.

Eventually, Marcus found himself speaking. 'Well, have you ever heard of **the third changing room?**' he asked.

'The third changing room?' Stacey repeated.

'You know, at Stillwater. That tiny stadium where we used to go and play football,' Marcus replied. 'Rumours are that there's a third changing room there.'

'What does that mean?' Lise said. Stacey nudged Marcus to continue.

'Football stadiums normally have two changing rooms, one for the home team, one for the away team. So three changing rooms would be **odd,**' Marcus went on, trying his best to make it all seem boring. He didn't want to set Stacey off on another rant about the supernatural, but she didn't buy it.

'*That sounds interesting!* That sounds *very* interesting,' she said.

'If we found the abandoned, secret third changing room, maybe that could be our hideout?' Marcus suggested.

'But wouldn't it still be a changing room?' Asim replied with a frown. 'Do we really want the **smell of feet** in our hideout?'

'Do you have anywhere better?' Marcus said.

Stacey scrunched up her face and then pulled out a messy notebook. 'I'll put it on the list for later.'

Lise spoke up next.

'I might know a place.' She raised her eyebrows conspiratorially. 'The storage space down the corridor, third door on the left, just before the fire exit. It was big enough for me and a couple of members of Robotics Club – we've snuck away tonnes of times to play **Zelda** on our Switches.'

Marcus was surprised. He hadn't taken Lise for the rule-breaking type – it seemed like he had more to learn about his teammates.

'I don't know if that's big enough for us —
we have four members,' Asim pointed out.

The bell for first class rang.

Marcus sighed. They hadn't got any
closer to finding out **what that
creature was,** finding a hideout or
finding his football.

'We're failing. I don't like failing,' Asim
said glumly. 'What happens now?'

'Don't give up hope, guys,' Stacey said.
'We're getting closer — we just need to keep
at it. Let's meet tomorrow and try to figure
something out.'

The group got up and began to leave.
Asim was right, Marcus thought. They
were **failing,** and worse than that they
were wasting time. They were going to wait

another day before meeting? That would only leave two days – and one of them was Saturday, when they wouldn't be at Breakfast Club. What if he never got his football back from the creature? *What if–*

A large hand landed on Marcus's shoulder, and he spun round to find Mr Anderson looking down at him.

'I heard you went under the fence,' he said.

Chapter Nine

'What were you thinking?' Mr Anderson said. He was sitting on a table and trying to meet Marcus's eyes, but Marcus was staring determinedly at his shoes. 'What would your mum think?'

'I know, I know,' Marcus breathed. He closed his eyes. 'I'm just – I'm just looking for something.'

'Listen, I understand. You don't have to

tell me anything. Just let me know if there's anything I can do to help. Oyin and Patrick seem to think you need help too,' said Mr Anderson.

An image of a ball **spinning away** from the tip of Marcus's boot sprang into his mind. 'Thanks, sir, but you can't help me,' he said. 'Neither can they.' He just needed to figure out what the creature was and **solve the mystery** of his football in time for Lola's return, then she would be able to help him get his touch back.

Mr Anderson shook his head. 'Maybe that's how it used to be, but that doesn't have to be how it is now.'

Marcus looked down again. Mr Anderson really didn't understand.

'Well,' Mr Anderson sighed, 'at least you

have that new friendship group of yours.'

'Yeah,' Marcus said. Then he caught himself. 'Wait, they're not my friends.'

'Sure they are. You all huddle together, talking intently. I've seen you a couple of times now – including about two minutes ago.' Mr Anderson smiled and smoothed his tweed jacket.

'**Please** don't tell Mrs Miller that you saw me with them this morning. **Please, sir,**' Marcus begged. Just for a moment, his football slipped his mind.

Mr Anderson chuckled. 'I understand looking for adventure, Marcus.' He paused, as if he was thinking about something. Then he walked over to the canteen door and pulled it open. Stacey, Lise and Asim were standing there, clearly eavesdropping.

They straightened up guiltily.

Mr Anderson raised his eyebrows, but his eyes were twinkling as he looked at the three of them. 'Tell you what,' he said thoughtfully. 'Meet me in my classroom after school, OK?' They all glanced at each other, before nodding. 'Wonderful,' Mr Anderson said, clasping his hands together. And he strode through the doors without another word.

They were running late for class so they didn't get a chance to talk about what Mr Anderson had said, and by the time Marcus entered Mr Anderson's classroom at three fifteen that afternoon his mind was whirring. Why did their teacher want to meet them?

Were they going to get told off again?

Marcus was the last one to enter the classroom. Mr Anderson smiled at him and said, 'Well, if you wouldn't mind following me,' and beckoned them back out of the door. Marcus, Stacey, Asim and Lise exchanged puzzled looks.

Mr Anderson led them down one of the corridors and all the way outside. Looking over his shoulder, he said, 'So a couple of the teachers and I used to be in a band.'

That's so cool!' said Lise. 'What did you play?'

They were trudging through the empty playground towards the school car park.

'Mostly jazz,' he replied. 'But something we always found difficult was finding a place for rehearsal. Somewhere away from teachers and students, where they wouldn't be able to hear us. We ended up settling on this place.' Mr Anderson pointed at the **small wooden building** in front of them. There was a heavy lock on its door.

Marcus had seen it before. All he knew was that the building belonged to someone important, and that students weren't supposed to mess with it.

'What is it?' asked Marcus uncertainly.

'A long time ago, there used to be grounds attached to the school. They were sold off, what with budget cuts, but the **groundskeeper's cabin** still remains,' Mr Anderson explained as he walked over to the padlock with a key. The door creaked open.

'*Whoa,*' Marcus breathed.

The cabin was small, but it managed to fit in a whole lot of items. There was a couch, a table, and even a couple of rickety wooden chairs.

'I wanted to show you this place because I think it will help you stay out of trouble,' Mr Anderson said solemnly. 'I know Mrs Miller has her eye on you lot, but I can see how much fun you're all having together at

Breakfast Club, and I want you to be able to continue that.' He paused. 'But I don't want you to do anything else dangerous. This place is safe, and it's on school property.'

'*This will be perfect,*' Stacey breathed as she slowly walked into the room.

'Thanks, Mr Anderson,' Lise said with a smile so big that her face could barely contain it.

'That's fine,' Mr Anderson said. He winked. 'Just don't tell Mrs Miller or anyone else that you got this from me, all right?'

'Of course, our lips are sealed, sir!' Stacey said. Mr Anderson beamed at them, then plopped the key down inside and left them in the cabin.

 Marcus leaped onto the couch, and a **cloud of dust** wafted up into his face.

Lise took a seat next to him. Asim perched on the edge of one of the wooden chairs, staring up at the walls.

'**WOW,** so I guess we have a hideout!' Stacey exclaimed. She punched the air in excitement.

The rest of the detectives whooped and cheered.

Chapter Ten

'If it's our hideout, shouldn't we do something to really make it *our* hideout?' Lise asked, staring around at the walls.

'What if we say that every person has to bring something to the hideout? Something to make the place ours.' The words had left Marcus's mouth before he'd even realized what he was saying.

'That sounds like a great idea,' Lise chirped.

'Super cool! Let's try to bring something tomorrow, OK?' Stacey said.

Asim nodded. Then he reached into his backpack and took out the chewed up, **slime-covered** Nintendo Switch. He placed it on the table at the centre of the room.

Stacey clambered up onto the table. 'Now, finally, we can talk about the next step of our investigation! **Finding the creature and getting our stuff back!**' Then she paused. 'But let's save it for tomorrow. It's getting late.' She clambered down.

Marcus's stomach dropped. 'What?' he said. 'I thought we were going to talk about it now!'

'There's no rush, Marcus—' Stacey tried to wave him off, but Marcus didn't stop talking.

'But there is. There is a rush.' He paused and glanced around at the other detectives.

'We have to find that creature! Don't you all want to get back the things that we lost? Don't you care?' What he really wanted to say was, *Don't you care about me getting my football back?*

Stacey gave him a hard stare. 'I care about today. And yesterday. And what we've been doing this week. That's what this is all about. Don't you even see that?'

There was silence.

Then Lise cleared her throat and began to talk. 'We do care, Marcus. It's just that it's not the **only** thing we care about. School finished ages ago. I need to get home, it's club recruitment day tomorrow and my parents will be worried if I'm out any later.'

'Yes, club recruitment day,' Stacey chimed in. 'We all need to go and look interested in other clubs. Keep Mrs Miller happy and off our tails.'

'I *am* interested in other clubs,' said Asim.

'Me too,' said Lise. 'I love **Robotics** and *Board-games Club* and—'

'That's it, team – just the right tone,' interrupted Stacey with a **big wink.** Asim and Lise just rolled their eyes.

Marcus's head dropped. He hadn't even thought of recruitment day, or how late it was getting. 'Sure, *fine,*' Marcus said. 'See you all tomorrow, then.' He trudged out of the hideout. He knew he was being difficult, but that didn't stop him from feeling annoyed. He needed to find a way to tell them why the football was so important to him, to really show them.

By the time he got back to his flat, he knew what he was going to bring to the hideout the next day.

Chapter Eleven

Breakfast Club the next morning was *buzzing* with energy. People sat around in groups, all making posters and signs for their own clubs to display at the recruitment day. Mr Anderson stood at the centre of the canteen directing traffic, making sure the paper, scissors and paint moved around the room, and that everything was shared fairly.

Club recruitment day was a **big deal** at Rutherford. Almost everyone belonged to one club or another, and there was no better way to make friends. It only came around twice a year, and club members spent ages creating stalls and cool activities to try to convince people to join. It was so popular that it ran during the school day, meaning that students got *a whole lesson off.*

The first two classes on club recruitment day were a struggle to get through. Marcus wasn't interested in joining any more clubs – he wasn't even sure he wanted to keep going to football without his touch – but the excitement of everyone around him was still infectious. Teachers found it difficult to keep their classes focused, and the level of conversation was steadily rising with each passing minute. Then, finally, it was lunchtime, and after that it began.

'Do you want to look around at the other

clubs?' Marcus asked Oyin and Patrick when they had managed to push their way through the packed canteen and eaten their lunch. Kids were rushing past them now, trying to be first to either set up their stalls or go to see other people's.

'Nah, sorry, we're in charge of the Football Club's stall,' Oyin said.

'We're first years, so they made us do it.' Patrick rolled his eyes.

Marcus's eyebrows **scrunched up.** 'What about me? I'm a first year!'

'Well, you're not really playing right n—' Oyin was interrupted by a stiff elbow from Patrick.

'They asked for you to do it too. We're, er, just being nice and taking over for you,' Patrick said.

Marcus frowned. The truth was written all over Patrick's and Oyin's faces. He hadn't been to any training sessions in a month, and hadn't told the other members of the Football Club why. They must have thought he just didn't want to go any more. **Marcus wasn't surprised.**

'OK,' he finally said. The word pained his chest. 'Cool.'

'Look around, enjoy the other stalls,' Patrick said. 'See you later!' And he and Oyin walked off out of the canteen to set up their stall.

Marcus sighed. There was only a day and a half left – but if he didn't find that creature then he wouldn't find his football. Then he'd have to tell Lola he'd lost it, then she'd never help him get his touch back, and then it was **over.** By the time the next club recruitment day rolled round he'd have to look for a new club, but he wasn't sure he was good at much else. And without Football Club he'd have less in common with Oyin and Patrick — he'd be the odd one out. Then they'd stop talking to him and he'd be all **alone** at school. Marcus swallowed, his

throat feeling suddenly dry.

The BCI needed to work out what that creature was. That was the first step. Everything else would make sense after that – Marcus was sure. He let out a frustrated sigh. All he wanted was to be with the BCI in their hideout, working on the case.

For now, he just had to get through club recruitment day. He knew that all he had to do was make it look as if he was interested in other things. Throw Mrs

Miller *off their scent* so they could get back to the investigation. He could do that, right?

The canteen was now practically deserted. Marcus pushed thoughts of the creature and his football out of his head, and went into the school hall where club recruitment day was in full swing.

Desks had been lifted out of classrooms and placed throughout the hall. They were covered with fairy lights and most had mini speakers playing music. It was like a **giant** collision of all kinds of colours, lights and music. Sign-up forms were on every desk with multiple pens at the ready. Posters fluttered as students bustled past them. Club members called out to anyone who even looked in the direction of their stalls.

It was **kind of a mess,** and Marcus loved it.

He could see Oyin and Patrick at the Football Club stall, and Lise at the Board-games Club stall next to it, taking signatures. As Marcus watched, she walked over to the Robotics Club stall to help them set up. When Marcus next looked, Lise was somehow at the Cooking Club stall.

Marcus chuckled and walked over to talk to her, intrigued.

'Why are you at so many club stalls?' he asked when he arrived.

'Oh, hi, Marcus.' Lise smiled. 'I have a lot of clubs that I'm a member of.' She said it as if it was the most obvious thing in the world.

'But how can you do it with all the —' Marcus lowered his voice — 'you know, the

BCI stuff?' Marcus said 'BCI' in a whisper, glancing around for Mrs Miller.

'Well, this week has been the busiest BCI has been all year,' Lise said. 'Before, it was more of an odd occasional hobby. Stacey only started at Rutherford after Christmas, remember? And I only met up with her and worked on cases like . . . once a month? I wanted to meet up more – it was all so fascinating – but Stace would always put it off.' Lise leaned against the wall, and tucked her hair behind her ear.

'Why?'

'I don't know. I guess it felt like she was more focused on research, like she was always searching for that *perfect* case,' she admitted.

'And you waited? You didn't leave the club?' Marcus asked.

'I didn't want to miss out.' Lise grinned. 'I don't like missing out. It's why I end up joining all these clubs.' She chuckled, then fell silent as Mrs Miller strode past where they were standing.

Marcus's chest began to pound. Then a thought suddenly occurred to him. 'Wait – when Mrs Miller hauled us into her office she already knew about the BCI! **How?**' He lowered his voice. 'I thought it was secret.'

'It's our investigations that are supposed to be secret, not the BCI itself – I mean, we made a banner. And, well, that wasn't the first time that we've been called to her office,' Lise whispered. 'Despite us not spending that much time on our previous cases, well . . . BCI investigations can get a little bit **out of control.'**

'I can see that,' Marcus said, thinking about what they had done in less than a week.

'It's never gone this far before, though.' Marcus noticed that Lise's usual smile was still on her face, but there was something nervous about it now. 'This mystery is pushing Stace. **It didn't used to be like this . . .** Anyway, I have to get back to my stalls. I'll see you later at the hideout.' Lise walked off, leaving Marcus with more questions than he'd had before. Then he smiled. The hideout, **solving the mystery,** figuring out what that creature was – Marcus couldn't wait to get back to it.

He kept walking around the busy fair, and eventually found himself near the Art Club's stall. Asim sat alone at the edge of the desk.

His earbuds were in and he was sketching

something. Marcus noticed that the other people manning the stall would occasionally sneak glances at him, but they didn't say anything.

As Marcus approached, he could make out their voices.

'Why do we even have him here? He doesn't help us with anything,' a boy with dark curls said, rolling his eyes.

'He's even been **sneaking off** recently,' replied the tall girl he was standing next to.

'Maybe he'll leave. That would be a good outcome,' the boy sneered.

'No way. He's always making art. He's not leaving the club, it's all he has.'

'Then what's up with him? What is he doing? What is he hiding?' the boy asked. There was a harsh edge to his voice.

What is he hiding? Marcus shook his head. His face felt **hot.** How could they think that about Asim? And what was it based on? Just that he went off to hang out with the BCI every once in a while? Marcus couldn't believe they were being so unkind.

Before they could say anything else, Marcus cut through the crowd, walking straight towards the Art Club stall.

'Hey,' Marcus blurted out when he got there. The boy's and girl's heads whipped round to look at him. Asim hadn't noticed him approach, and carried on drawing with his earbuds in.

'What's up? Are you here to join the club?' the girl said.

'You shouldn't talk like that about Asim,' Marcus said in a forceful whisper.

The Art Club members looked shocked. Then the boy scoffed, 'You don't know what you're talking about.'

Marcus shook his head firmly. 'Yes, I do. We can't make assumptions about people just because they're a little different from us. *Asim's a good guy.* Don't talk about him that way.' Breathing heavily, Marcus turned on his heel and stormed off before the club members could say another word.

'Stupid,' Marcus muttered underneath his breath as he walked away, thinking about what the Art Club had said.

What's up with him?

Those same doubts had formed in Marcus's head, just because Asim was a little bit quiet and had seemed a little bit odd. Was Marcus just as bad as the people in the Art Club? He frowned. Maybe he had been as bad as them, but he knew that he didn't have to be any more.

Marcus shook his head. Asim, Lise and Stacey were all full of surprises. And Marcus knew that they were his best chance of getting his football back, and solving this mystery.

Chapter Twelve

The moment Marcus saw the hideout after school, he knew something was **wrong.** He was approaching it from across the car park, and he could see Stacey, Lise and Asim all standing in front of the wooden building, but for some reason they weren't going in. He slung his backpack over his shoulder and started to run towards them as fast as he could. As he got nearer, the sound of his own footsteps was drowned out by a louder, harsher noise.

Stacey, Lise and Asim didn't even look at him when he skidded to a halt next to them. They were all staring at the hideout with wide eyes. Loud **crashing** and **bangs** were coming from inside.

'Er, what's going on?' Marcus said, trying to make himself heard over a particularly loud clanging sound. 'What's making that noise?'

'I think,' Stacey said in a hushed voice, 'that we may have a ghost here.'

'Wh-what if this place is haunted by the ghost of the groundskeeper?' Asim said, taking a step back.

All four of them were silent as the noises from inside the cabin intensified.

'But it can't really be that, right?' Marcus

said, looking at Lise for support. 'Look, I'm sure there's a completely normal explanation for this.'

None of them would meet his eye; they continued to stare avidly at the shaking cabin.

'We have to see what's in there,' Marcus insisted. When none of them replied, he very cautiously approached the door. As he got closer, sweat began to prickle on his forehead. *What if it really was a ghost?*

BANG!

The door shook, sending a puff of dust into the air.

Marcus stopped walking.

BANG!

The door shook again, its wooden panels bulging out at odd angles.

Marcus's heart was pounding so hard that it felt almost as loud as the banging on the door in front of him.

BANG!

The door of the hideout burst open, and a huge creature tore through it. It moved so quickly that Marcus could barely see it, but he recognized it as the same beast they'd seen in the empty supermarket.

Marcus fell back, away from the thing, yelling. He heard the others shouting behind him too.

But, before they could decide what to do, the beast leaped away from them in one *giant bound* and sped across the playground, vanishing into the distance.

'That was not a ghost,' Marcus said, his voice shaking as he lifted himself from the ground. 'That was **definitely** not a ghost.'

This beast was something else, something he'd never even heard of before.

'No, definitely not a ghost . . .' Stacey repeated. Her usual confident voice was gone, replaced with something quieter and much more unsure.

No one spoke for a moment.

'You know, after the first time we saw it, I kept thinking that maybe it was all in my head. That we'd just seen a dog or something,' Lise said. Her eyes were wide behind her glasses. 'But that thing, it's real, isn't it?'

What are we doing here?' Asim whispered, his voice full of terror. 'Are we sure that we can go up against that thing?'

'Yes. We have to,' Marcus said, dusting himself off. He took a deep breath and stepped through the broken door, even though his legs were still shaking.

The inside of the hideout was in a similar state to its front door. Chairs had been thrown to the ground and the couch had been **torn up.** Springs and stuffing poked out of its fabric. The table lay on its side. There was debris all over the floor, and Marcus could make out **scratch marks** on the wall. Covering everything, there was a clear, slimy substance that he recognized from the supermarket. It was the **ectoplasm.**

He swallowed. His chest felt as if someone had made a hole in it. He turned away from the mayhem and met the eyes of his fellow detectives. They didn't have to say anything. Marcus knew how they were feeling.

But then Marcus noticed something else.

Above the ruined couch, in bright bold colours, four words had been painted onto the wall:

THE BREAKFAST CLUB INVESTIGATORS

'Asim, did you do this?' Lise said in awe, stepping over the broken chairs with a beaming smile on her face.

'Well, who else could?' Asim said with a shrug. 'This place needed a little touch-up. We said that we were going to bring things, so I brought this. I just came into

school early this morning and worked on it. Not that it matters now, because everything got trashed . . .' He trailed off.

'WOW, that must have taken a lot of time,' Stacey said. She leaned over the couch and reached out to touch it.

THE BREAKFAST CLUB INVESTIGATORS

'Well, my mum's an artist, she taught me how to do murals. It took a bit of time but – you know,' Asim finished modestly.

'But still, Asim, this is *amazing!*' Marcus said. He smiled at Asim, but Asim looked away.

'It's the Breakfast Club Investigators. I . . . well, I feel like I belong here. I've never belonged somewhere before. So this is a small thing to do for us,' he mumbled. 'I mean, you're all helping me find what I lost – and it's something that means a lot to me. It's –' he took a deep breath – 'a notebook of my mum's paintings.'

'So *that's* what you lost,' Marcus said.

'Yeah, someone threw it over the fence into that alleyway. When I tried to get it back it was gone. Just like your football, Marcus,'

Asim said, lowering his eyes.

'Asim, I'm sorry, that's . . .' Marcus trailed off.

'Really unfair!' Stacey exclaimed. 'But don't worry, Asim – we'll find it,' she finished confidently.

'Yeah, we're like a real-life detective group now, right?' Marcus said.

'We sure are,' Lise replied. All four of them grinned at each other.

Just for a second, Marcus wasn't thinking about how he only had about a day left to get his football. He was thinking about the people in the messy, broken room with him and how he wanted to share something with them.

Sitting down on a torn cushion on the floor, Marcus reached into his backpack and pulled out a stone. The stone was just a little smaller than his fist, oval shaped with smooth sides, and a deep almost-purple colour.

He took a **deep breath.**

'The first time I travelled for a holiday was last summer. Lola, my cousin, had been living with us for a while after her mum – my mum's sister – passed away. We all got into the car and went down to the seaside. Lola's the one who persuaded Mum. She said that we had to do it before she left, that playing football on the beach would make us feel better. She's really good at football, **way** better than me. She got a scholarship to play at college in America, so she'd been training really hard all last summer, but she said playing beach football would improve her control. And she was right.

'Have you ever played football on the

beach? **It's so hard!** Your feet are slipping and sliding all over the place, and you can barely keep balance. And any time you try to run your feet **sink** into the sand. It's so tiring to move.' As Marcus spoke, he could almost feel the sand in between his toes. 'Even with all of that, she was *amazing,* pulling out rabonas and Cruyff turns all over the place. I think that was the best that I've ever seen her play. Then, once we were done playing, she gave me her ball – *the* ball – and said, "I can't take this on the plane – take care of it for me so we can have a kickabout when I'm home." And then I lost it.'

'I'm sorry,' Asim blurted out suddenly. He looked uneasy.

Marcus looked at him, confused. 'For what?'

'I guess I just thought it was a silly football,' Asim admitted.

'The things we lost, they're all **more than that,'** Stacey said wisely, catching everyone's eyes.

Marcus nodded, then continued the story. 'Well, when we were done playing football, we'd sit by the water and **skip stones.** This was the final stone I was supposed to throw before I left on the last day. But I never threw it. So here it is.' Marcus knew he was supposed to drop the stone on one of the intact shelves, but he couldn't let go of it, just like he hadn't been able to let go of it back then. It felt as though if he did, he'd never see Lola again.

'Why didn't you throw it?' Lise said.

'It's silly,' Marcus muttered with his head down.

'You can still tell us.' Stacey rested a hand on his shoulder.

Marcus took a deep breath. 'Deep down, I think I thought that if I didn't throw it, that maybe the holiday wouldn't end, but it still did.'

'But it's not over,' Lise said. There was this look in her eyes, soft but determined. 'The story you just told, the stone, it's all right here. **It isn't over.'**

Marcus nodded, even though he didn't quite understand. 'What did the rest of you bring?' he asked, wanting to move the conversation away from him.

'I brought a book,' Stacey replied. She rummaged around in her backpack, then she brandished a thick book and handed it over to Marcus. Asim and Lise picked their way through the slime-covered mess to look at it over his shoulder. The cover and pages were wrinkled and worn. It looked as if it had been read hundreds of times.

Marcus read out the title.

'AN
ENCYCLOPAEDIA
OF THE
SUPERNATURAL.'

The front cover had illustrations of a **werewolf**, a **vampire** and a **ghost.**

'Yep,' said Stacey, sounding pleased with herself. 'Bound to be useful in our line of work.'

'It's a bit **battered**,' Asim said, poking the dog-eared pages.

'My dad used to read it to me when I was a kid. And I've read it more than a couple times – I had the free time when I moved here, after all . . .' Stacey trailed off. 'I didn't really have any friends or anything over here. Everything was new, so I needed something old. And I've been using it to try to figure out what this creature actually is.'

'Find anything useful?' Lise asked hopefully.

'I did, actually,' Stacey said, her eyes shining. 'This mythical creature is –' she paused dramatically –

'a chupacabra.'

It felt as if a cold breeze had blown through the room. Marcus, Lise and Asim all shivered.

'A chupawhatnow?' Marcus asked.

'A chupa*cabra*,' Stacey said, as if it was the most obvious thing in the world.

'It sounds terrifying,' Asim said with a shake of his head.

'Exactly! And what it *is* is **terrifying** too. It's a **hairless beast** that walks around on four legs and it sucks the blood of goats.' Stacey used her hand to mime a chupacabra walking around then jumping on her other hand, which was apparently pretending to be goat.

'Whoa, that's like a **vampire dog!** I don't want to get caught up with that.'

Lise wrapped her arms round her body.

'I'm not sure . . .' Marcus said slowly. 'Do chupacabras actually exist? And, even if they do, we don't have goats anywhere near here, so why would a chupacabra be here?' Marcus glanced down at the book in Stacey's hands. 'And – look – it says that chupacabras live in America!'

The room fell silent. Then Stacey began to talk again. 'Well, that's just another part of the mystery for us to solve. What **evil plans** does the chupacabra have? What plane did it catch to get here?'

All four of them laughed.

'I'm next!' Lise said, lifting her hand. 'So I brought this for us.' She waved a small plastic device in the air.

'Is that a fan?' Marcus said.

'Yeah, it's a USB fan that I made. I thought it'd be useful for when we get hot.' Lise looked very self-satisfied.

'Wait, you made that, all by yourself?' Marcus asked. There was an exposed wire or two, but other than that Marcus would have thought that Lise had bought it in a store.

'But it's spring right now – it's not hot at all,' Asim pointed out.

'I know, but it'll be summer in a month or two, and hopefully we'll still be here in this hideout trying to **solve cases.** That's what we all want, right?' Lise said, looking around eagerly.

Stacey glanced up from her book. Marcus felt a warm feeling in his chest, but it was tinged with something else. **Guilt.** He was only here for his football. He hadn't really thought about what came after.

'Maybe. Let's just solve this case first, all right?' Marcus said. He shook his head. What was he doing? There was only a day left to find his football. 'To start with, we have to look around this mess for clues.'

Chapter Thirteen

The group immediately started to search around the debris, their minds firmly back on the investigation.

'We didn't even need to go and find it; it came to us!' Stacey said from the floor. *'This is amazing!'*

'The biggest question is, how did it know we were here?' Marcus asked, picking up some cushion feathers. The ectoplasm made them stick to his hand. **'Ugh!'**

'Is it tracking us? Can it find us?' Asim's face was pale. 'What type of creature can do that?'

'The Nintendo Switch is gone,' Lise said suddenly.

They all stopped what they were doing to look at each other.

Marcus swallowed.

What did that mean?

This mystery was getting stranger and stranger.

'I used to have a cat when I was younger,' Stacey said slowly. 'It loved sleeping on one of my jumpers, and no matter where I hid it the cat always knew where the jumper was.'

'What does that have to do with the creature?' Marcus asked, confused.

'Cats have a much more **powerful sense of smell than humans.** It smelled my jumper.' A grin broke out across Stacey's face.

'So, are you saying . . .' Marcus started.

'The chupacabra *smelled* the Switch! *That's* how it found our hideout and *that's* why the Switch is the only thing missing. It took the Nintendo Switch back to its den,' Lise said, putting it all together.

'It tracked us that far?' Asim said in a small voice. 'What type of thing could track us that far?'

'**A chupacabra, of course!**' Stacey exclaimed.

'That is more than a little creepy,' Marcus said.

'But it's useful – if we know it can track things, then we can set a **trap** for it!' Stacey rubbed her hands together.

'Set a trap for it? Do we want to get eaten? Look what it did to the hideout!' Asim stood up, gesturing to the mess all around them.

'We have to,' Stacey said decisively. 'And I have a secret weapon. Something that means we'll definitely be able to find all the things we've lost.' That grin surfaced again. She looked across the room at Lise.

Asim and Marcus looked round at Lise too. She sighed. 'I've been building a tracker since we first saw the creature. That's what Stace is talking about. If it works, we could put it on the chupacabra and then follow it back to its home . . .' Lise trailed off. 'But it's not ready yet.'

'You can make a tracker? **That's wild!**' Marcus exclaimed. He felt as if he was learning something new about Lise every day.

'More like I can make adjustments to things I already have in the house.' Lise scratched the back of her head.

'That's still very *cool.*' Asim was looking at Lise with wonder in his eyes.

'You can get it ready tonight, though, right?' Stacey nudged Lise with her elbow.

'Maybe. It might be possible,' she said.

'**Then let's do it!**' Marcus said.

'I don't know . . .' Asim murmured.

'Don't you want to get your mum's book

of paintings back?' Marcus said sharply. Asim stiffened, but Marcus pushed on. 'This is the only way we're going to get it, so are you in or are you out?'

'I guess I don't really have a choice,' Asim muttered.

'None of us do,' Stacey said, rolling up her sleeves. **'We're detectives.** We have to follow this to the end.'

'Do we?' Lise said hesitantly. 'Isn't it all getting a bit dangerous, Stace?' Lise wasn't normally the scared type, but she looked nervous right now. Marcus opened his mouth, but didn't really know what to say. Lise wasn't being unreasonable – she was right, this was dangerous.

'There's one **big hole** in this plan, though,' Asim pointed out. 'How do we even get the chupacabra to come back again? The Nintendo Switch is gone.'

They all fell silent. Stacey sat on the sofa and put her face in her hands, thinking. 'We need something to replace the Switch,' she said, her voice slightly muffled. 'Something else that the chupacabra took, but accidentally left behind.'

'Or we need the closest thing to that,' Marcus said. **'Look at all this ectoplasm!'**

Stacey's head jerked up in excitement.

'So, if we rub that over something, like old trainers –' Marcus had a set of trainers with multiple holes in them that came into his mind as he talked – 'then maybe that works as **bait.'**

'But how to do we get the tracker on it?'

Asim said, running a hand through his hair. 'Can we just – I don't know – throw it on?'

'No,' Lise said immediately. 'It needs to be clipped on.'

'That means we need to **trap it,** even if it's just for a couple of seconds,' Stacey replied. 'We could try a cage, but where are we going to get a cage that big?'

'What about a cage of cloth? My parents have a bunch of old extra-large bedsheets that they used to use to stop paint getting everywhere. If we could tie it up in one of them, then maybe it might work,' Asim said.

'It'd only contain the chupacabra for a *couple of seconds,* but maybe that's enough.' Stacey was grinning again now.

'With the tracker on, we'd just have to follow it to its nest. We could do that easily,'

Lise said, nodding quickly, her blonde hair bobbing around her head.

The four of them looked at each other in excitement. Marcus's heart leaped. He was so close to getting his football back.

Chapter Fourteen

The next day, the tracker was ready, and the Breakfast Club Investigators were in the forest behind their school setting up their trap.

The beaten-up trainers were at the centre of a small clearing, with a large bedsheet underneath them. Each corner of the bedsheet had a piece of rope tied tight to it, and each rope looped up and over a nearby set of tree branches, and then back to the hands of each of the detectives.

Once the creature was on the material, all they had to do was *p u l l* their rope and then the bedsheet would **shoot up,** wrapping up whatever was in the middle of it. Marcus had tied his rope tight round his wrist. He wanted to make sure that no matter what happened, no matter how **scared** he got, he wouldn't let go.

'How's the tracker?' Marcus whispered to Lise. The two of them were lying next to each other on the forest floor, opposite Stacey and Asim. He pointed down at what looked like a paper clip fused with a small black plastic box, from which a blue light flashed every couple of seconds.

'I was up all last night working on it,' Lise said, her eyes bright. 'I think it's going to work.'

Marcus gave her a thumbs up. He felt the **energy** coursing through his body. They were going to find out what the creature was, and then it would lead them to his football. He was sure of it.

The ground was dry and hard, and riddled with stones. Marcus had to slightly change position every couple of minutes to stop the pins and needles in his legs. Each time he moved, he made a tiny bit of noise, which made Stacey *glare* at him across the clearing. She was alert, her eyes darting around at the smallest sign of movement or sound.

Lise and Asim were different, though. Marcus could tell they were **terrified** of seeing the creature again. It was almost as if they were making an effort to avoid looking at anything that might sound or look unusual. Next to him, Lise stayed completely still. **She didn't even move an inch.**

One hour later, however, Marcus was starting to get a little bored. He peered over the log he was hiding behind, checking that

Asim and Stacey were still there, just in time to see Asim's eyelids **slump** closed. Stacey glared at him but didn't actually elbow him until he started snoring.

'What if it doesn't show up?' Marcus murmured. He reached down by his feet and picked up his water bottle.

'It'll come. Even if it takes hours, it'll come,' Lise replied.

'Hours!' Marcus choked and spluttered out the water he was drinking.

'Shh,' came Stacey's furious whisper from across the clearing.

They were silent for a few more minutes. And then, suddenly, there was a rustle from behind a tree off to their left. Marcus turned, staring intently at the spot the sound had come from, but nothing happened.

Then there was a **rustle** from the right.

Marcus's head whipped round. But there was nothing there either. His heart was beating fast.

Something was coming – he could feel it.

Marcus closed his eyes for a moment.

'Did you hear that?' Lise whispered. She was sitting in the exact same position that she'd been in for the last hour. She hadn't even turned to look at the sound.

Marcus didn't reply. He couldn't. His eyes were fixed on the clearing, where the creature had just emerged.

The chupacabra. He caught a breath in his throat.

The chupacabra moved slowly but gracefully on its four dark, shiny legs. The steady **thump** of its paws on the ground was mirrored by the thump in Marcus's chest that got louder with every passing moment.

The creature's mouth hung open to reveal a **long dark tongue** and the very tips of **sharp** teeth. Its body wasn't as smooth as Marcus had thought before. It had a strange texture; it almost looked as if it was wet.

Its head sank low to the ground, and then one of its nostrils twitched. It was sniffing. It took a couple of slow steps one way, and then another. When it stepped on a branch, causing it to *snap,* the sound rang out in the silence like a bone breaking. Marcus jolted, accidentally kicking a stone.

As it skipped away, the chupacabra froze, its head swinging left then right. It looked directly at the hollowed-out, fallen tree that

Marcus and Lise were hiding behind. Marcus put his hand over his nose and mouth, too scared to take a breath, and lay as still as he could. Lise **shivered** next to him, her hands covering her face.

After a long minute, the creature relaxed and started moving again. It went straight to the trainers and leaned down to pick them up in its mouth.

Stacey yelled their codeword.

'Orange!'

Marcus pulled on the rope in his hand with all his might. He saw Lise do the same next to him.

The sheet sprang up from underneath the chupacabra. It was supposed to wrap the creature up, giving them time to attach the tracker. But it didn't quite work out like that.

Before Marcus could really understand what was going on, the rope that was tied round his wrist tugged back, hard. He **screamed** as the force ripped him out of his hiding space, dragging him across the ground.

Chapter Fifteen

Marcus yelled for help as he was pulled left and then right along the forest floor. Air **whooshed** in his ears, blocking out all other sounds. Trees flew past his eyes, dried leaves and dirt **sprayed** up in his face. Exposed tree roots bruised his ribs and broken twigs clawed at his arms. Ahead of him, he could see the chupacabra, running fast through the forest. Its head was covered by the sheet, but its body was completely free. The chupacabra must have moved just before their trap was sprung, and it was now *pulling* Marcus through the forest.

Marcus frantically reached up and tried to untangle his wrist from the rope. He gritted his teeth. Stretching up to it put even more pressure on his bruised chest, and the skin on his wrist was already **raw** with rope burn. But it was useless – the rope had been pulled too tight.

He looked up and saw the creature leap to one side to avoid a tree, but at such an angle that Marcus was heading straight for it. He threw his hand up over his eyes and waited for the **crash.**

Miraculously, it never came. Instead, he abruptly came to a stop.

Marcus lowered his arms. His nose was just a hair's breadth away from the tree trunk. He didn't wait to see why they had stopped, but immediately reached over to his trapped hand to untie the rope from his wrist. Then he **crawled** forward, wincing. He used the tree to pull himself back up to his feet, gazing at the chupacabra.

It was in the centre of a cluster of trees, **thrashing around,** yelping. The bedsheet was still wrapped round its head, but the ropes attached to it were pulled tight in all directions. It seemed they had got tangled on some of the branches, trapping the chupacabra.

He knew that this was their chance.

Marcus turned to see Lise running towards him, trailed by an unexpectedly *speedy* Stacey. Asim was jogging behind them.

Stacey bent over double when they finally reached Marcus. 'That may have been the fastest I've ever run,' she gasped. 'You OK?'

'Mostly.' Marcus forced a grin.

'That was **insane.** I don't know how you're still alive.' Asim walked in a circle round Marcus with wide eyes.

'Neither do I,' Marcus said. He clenched and then unclenched his fist, wincing as the blood rushed back to his fingers.

'Is that really it?' Lise whispered. She pointed at the chupacabra.

It howled and surged forward, causing the detectives to jump. The ropes kept the creature from escaping, but the slow cracks of the branches around it told them that they didn't have much time left.

Lise began to creep towards the chupacabra, each step silent and slow. Her entire body shook, but still she gripped the tracker tight. Marcus's heart was **thumping so hard** that it was all he could hear. Finally, trying hard to avoid its thrashing limbs, Lise lifted the tracker and quickly clipped it to the chupacabra's body.

It **howled** once more, and shook, throwing itself one way and then another. Lise backed away quickly, and the rest of the detectives scattered. All at once, the branches around the creature broke with a chorus of dry cracks.

The chupacabra was free.

For a moment it just stood there, almost as if it was surprised. The bedsheet had come off its head. It glanced over at them. The hair on Marcus's neck **stood up** and his breath caught in his throat. Then, without warning, it leaped through the forest, disappearing in the blink of an eye.

'Lise, did you get it?' Marcus cried as he rushed over.

'Yep,' Lise said as she brushed the dirt off her trousers. Stacey, Marcus and Asim all **high-fived** her, whooping and cheering.

'All right, let's go find this chupacabra!' Stacey cried.

Lise reached into her backpack and pulled out a small tablet, bringing up an app with a cat icon.

'This is an app for cats?' Asim asked, eyebrow raised.

'I made some changes to the cat tracker we had at home,' Lise replied. 'Cats, chupacabras – same difference.'

Asim chuckled.

'Hey, if it does the job, it does the job,' Marcus said. 'It'll work out, right, Lise?'

Lise smiled at Marcus before typing a code into the app, bringing up a radar on the screen. 'It looks like it's this way.' Lise pointed back towards their school. They all looked at each other in determination, and then began to walk there.

The radar led them out of the forest, and back onto the streets.

People stared at them. Marcus didn't really understand why until he noticed

they were all covered in dirt.
Him in particular. And Lise's hands were stained with something dark and shiny, almost like oil, but Marcus couldn't work out what it was.

'This way,' Lise said, pointing the group down an alley. Marcus followed her, looking around. The further they went into it, the more he had an **odd feeling.** He'd been here before, in this very alleyway. He was sure of it. He used to walk through here with Oyin and Patrick. But why . . . ?

'We're almost there. It should be right ahead of us,' Lise said excitedly.

She stopped in front of a large skip, filled to the brim with rubbish. It was giving off a very **unpleasant smell.** Next to it was a big barrel full of a black oily liquid, and there were black stains splattered all over the ground.

'I don't see any sign of that creature here,' Marcus murmured. He shook his head, but didn't say any more. He didn't even want to consider that they might have lost the chupacabra. The adrenaline in his veins had long ago run dry, and he felt **sore** all over from having been dragged across the forest floor.

'Maybe it's hiding in the skip?' Lise suggested. 'Asim, give me a leg up.' Lise passed the tablet to Stacey and then Asim hoisted her into the skip.

Stacey watched, her nose wrinkled. Lise reached out to pick up some of the rubbish and sniffed it gingerly. **'Ugh!'** she exclaimed.

'You think it's hiding underneath all that

rubbish?' Marcus shook his head again.
'I think I'll leave that to you.'

There was a rustling and then a great **thud**
from the skip. Marcus glanced up. Lise's legs
were in the air.

'I think I slipped on something really bad,'
she said, her voice muffled.

'Rather you than me!' Stacey said. 'That's weird, though. Why is the tracker saying that the chupacabra should be right –' she pointed forcefully at the ground **'here?'**

'Maybe it's broken,' Asim suggested.

'It can't be. I tested it so many times,' Lise said, righting herself and eventually jumping off the skip. Everyone around took a step back at the smell. 'And I've already turned the app off and on again. Look.' Lise walked over to Asim and Stacey. Both **recoiled** slightly at the smell.

Marcus walked around, keeping his eyes trained on the floor, tuning out the sound of Lise trying to force the others to look at her tablet and stop calling her **smelly.** And then he saw it.

'I think I understand,' Marcus said quietly. When the others didn't stop squabbling, he said again, louder, 'I get it! I know why the tracker led us here!'

The other three fell silent as he reached down and lifted the tracker from the floor.

'Because it's here.'

Stacey walked over to him and peered at the tracker. 'It must've fallen off when the chupacabra ran through here,' she said.

'We're not going to be able to find it now, are we?' Lise said. Her head dropped.

'No,' Asim replied. The word crumbled as it left his lips.

'But we can try again,' Stacey said fiercely. She looked at each one of them in turn, trying to catch their eyes, as if the confidence she felt would be transferred to them if only they would look at her.

Marcus didn't meet her eyes. Neither did Asim. But, after a moment, Lise looked up. 'We know how to attract it – we just have to do it again, but better this time. We can do that, right?' No one responded. A grim mood had descended on the detectives.

Marcus glanced up at the skip once more. Beneath the rubbish, something stood out to him.

'Wait . . . is that what I think it is?' he exclaimed. He didn't wait for anyone to respond – he just scrambled up into the skip and began clearing things out the way: a full nappy, a moth-eaten rug, some **mouldy** takeaway . . .

And then he could reach it. It was a little

flat, but unmistakable. He yanked it into the air. *It's my football* – I can't believe it! My football's here!' Marcus yelled. He jumped down from the skip and **punched** the air. A great welling of emotion washed through him. His last chance and he had finally found it!

Stacey clambered up onto the skip and looked inside. **'This can't be it,'** she murmured after a couple of seconds.

'This can't be what?' Marcus replied absent-mindedly. He was already off in his head, imagining Lola playing football with him, showing him how to fix his touch.

'There aren't enough things here; it's not the Chupacabra's nest.' Stacey got down, shaking her head. 'It must have just dropped the football here accidentally. No one else's stuff seems to be here.'

'But what did you lose, Stacey? We can take a look in the skip later.' Marcus wasn't even looking at her. He was doing **keepy-uppies** with his football, his eyes bright with glee.

'I didn't . . .' Stacey spoke so quietly that Marcus barely heard her.

Marcus kicked the ball wrong, and it tumbled to the floor. **'C'mon, Stacey.** Why don't you tell us what you lost?' he asked again.

'I didn't lose anything, OK? I don't have anything to get back from the chupacabra.' Stacey's voice was strained.

Marcus stared at her. 'Then why are you here?' he asked. Asim and Lise were watching the two of them awkwardly.

Stacey's face dropped. There was a hurt

look in her eyes. 'You really don't know?'

'No,' Marcus replied in a flat voice.

'Then you're stupid.' The words burst out of Stacey's mouth.

Marcus's eyebrows bunched up. His ears felt hot. 'You know what?' he said. 'That's fine. I'll just take my football and go home. I'm **done** here anyway; I was only part of this group to get my football back.'

'But the mystery isn't over. We still need to find the chupacabra and find out what it is and get the rest of everyone's stuff back,' Lise said, looking between Marcus and Stacey nervously. 'We should stick together.'

'Should we?' Asim murmured. 'I don't know.'

'I don't think so,' Marcus said, crossing his arms over his chest.

'Maybe you should leave, then,' Stacey snapped back.

Without responding, Marcus picked up his football, spun round and walked away from Stacey, Lise and Asim.

Chapter Sixteen

Marcus kicked the football. The first touches he made were small, little taps that sent the ball this way and that. Then he was hitting it a little harder. The football **thundered** off the wall and spun back at him, too fast for him to handle. It **cannoned** off his toe and disappeared behind him. Marcus groaned.

He slouched off to collect the ball from

where it had settled, underneath a car.

He was in a space on his estate just to the left of the recycling bins, a space that had always been his. He'd always used it to practise, but now things weren't going as well as they usually did.

He was sure that this had once been easier.

Maybe it was just that the football wasn't properly pumped? But he'd pumped it up a few times now, so surely that couldn't be the problem.

Or was it all those thoughts *buzzing* around his head? When he closed his eyes, that morning's argument with the Breakfast Club Investigators just kept replaying itself, over and over again. That look in Stacey's eye. The slow, fracturing smile on Lise's face. He'd hurt them, and he didn't like that.

Marcus shook the thoughts away. There wasn't anything he could do about it now, *right?*

All he could do was wait for Lola to arrive. She'd get him back on track, and that was all he needed, because that's how things had always been.

Marcus picked up the football and walked back up the stairs. He opened the door to his flat and immediately heard the sound of voices. He could make out his mum's voice, and another one that was *familiar but unfamiliar* at the same time. Marcus followed the sound through to the kitchen.

'Hey, Marcus.' Lola sat at the table next to a suitcase. '*Wow,* you've grown.' She gave a toothy grin. She was still taller than him, but not by much any more. Her braids were tied up into a ponytail, and she looked lean and strong. It'd only been six months, but it felt like so much longer.

'Of course he has – I've been feeding him,' Marcus's mum said proudly.

Marcus stared at his cousin in shock. **'Lola!** What—? Mum, what's she doing here?' He could hardly get any words out.

'Surprise!' Lola stood up to give him a tight hug. 'I got here a few hours early.' Her voice had a slight American twang to it now. **Marcus raised his eyebrow** – that was different.

'Well, I need to get some things from the shops.' Marcus's mum squeezed past them on her way to the front door. 'I'll leave you two to catch up.'

'You good?' Lola said as the door closed. She walked over to the living room and collapsed down into the couch. 'What've you been up to? How's the first half of year seven been? I can't believe I haven't been here for any of it! Made any new friends?'

Marcus followed her, taking the opportunity to look at her from different angles. He couldn't *believe* she was really here.

'No,' Marcus said. 'Well, maybe – I mean . . .' He trailed off.

'I think I know how that feels.' Lola gave him a tight smile. 'The football team at my college is pretty good, but it's super competitive, especially with that scholarship, so it was hard for me to make friends at first.' She paused. 'But things are much better now.' She grinned broadly. 'So, do you want to tell me about your new frien—?'

'I have the football.' The words spilled out of Marcus's mouth as he cut her off.

'The football?' Lola asked, looking confused.

'The one you gave me when you left,' Marcus said. The tips of his ears were starting to feel hot.

'Ah, **that football!** You still have it? I thought you would have moved on to another one by now – it's a bit old,' Lola said absent-mindedly.

'No, it's not. It's great,' Marcus insisted. His ears felt as if they were on fire now. He had to take a deep breath before he spoke again. 'Do you wanna go outside and play a little?'

'Maybe not right now – I'm still a little tired from the flight – but we definitely will soon,' Lola responded, smiling through a dramatic **yawn.**

Marcus forced a smile onto his face. 'Sure,' he said.

Once Marcus's mum got back from the shops, the three of them had dinner at their small table. It felt just like the old days, but at the same time it felt different.

'This is so good!' Lola said, helping herself to more potatoes. 'Thank you so much, Aunty. I've been missing your home cooking.'

The smile on Marcus's mum's face widened. 'Oh, well, after a long trip we have to make sure you're eating well.' She sounded pleased.

'No, seriously, this is the best thing I've eaten in months. It's *amazing,* isn't it, Marcus?' Lola said. But Marcus wasn't listening. He couldn't get the feeling that something was different and wrong out of his head. His fork absent-mindedly circled the edge of his plate as he tried to think of what it was. 'Isn't it, Marcus?' Lola said a little more loudly this time.

Marcus's head shot up. '*Huh?* Oh, yeah, great,' he muttered.

Marcus didn't hear the rest of his mum's and Lola's conversation. He'd retreated back inside himself, sitting with the slowly building feeling that something was wrong. But he just couldn't put his finger on what.

Marcus went to sleep frustrated a couple of hours later. He'd been waiting for Lola to come back for so long, but it hadn't been anything like he'd expected. She didn't want to have a kick around with him, and she didn't even remember the football. What was going on?

Chapter Seventeen

Marcus woke up in the middle of the night to the sound of his front door closing. He *crept* out of bed and stood in the corridor in his pyjamas, glancing left and right. The lights inside were off, but soft light from the street lamps outside lit the flat in a gentle glow. Marcus could just about see down the corridor, but no one was there.

He crept into the living room and saw that the sofa bed that Lola normally slept on was *empty*. That was weird. He could hear his mum snoring in her bedroom. Marcus walked over to the front door and opened it.

A soft, echoey, rhythmic thump came every couple of seconds. What *was* that? A gust of wind breezed by, and Marcus began to **shiver.**

The conversations he'd had with Stacey about **vampires** popped into his head. What if they *were* real? What if they'd taken Lola? What if they were the source of that weird sound?

Marcus grabbed his coat and his trainers and went outside. He followed the sound down the stairs. The closer he got, the more he began to recognize the **thumping** sound.

It was a football hitting a wall.

He found Lola kicking a ball against the wall over and over again. Marcus couldn't help but admire her technique. Each touch of the ball was perfect. She made it look easy. This was exactly what Marcus needed!

'Sorry if I woke you,' Lola said to Marcus, without even having to turn her head to see him. 'Maybe it's jet lag or something, but

I just couldn't get to sleep. Wanna join in?' The ball bounced off the wall and settled underneath her foot, and she **expertly** flicked her foot forward. The ball slowly rolled over to Marcus and stopped at his feet. He hadn't seen this one before. He looked down at it, but didn't make any move to kick it back to her.

'Why aren't you using our football?' Marcus swallowed hard and clenched his fists. 'The football *you* gave me?'

Lola raised her eyebrows. 'What's so important about it?' she asked in a soft voice.

What's so important about it? You really don't know? Marcus wanted to ask. But he didn't. He remembered that Stacey had said that to him earlier. Now he understood how much a question can hurt.

'I thought you were going to teach me everything, all your moves, but you just left.' Almost before he knew what he was saying, the words flooded out of his mouth. 'I've been waiting for you, you know. *I lost my touch*. I've even stopped playing football, because I wanted you to help me. I've been waiting for you to teach me.' Marcus kicked Lola's ball, sending it spinning off into the night. 'And you don't even remember the football – you told me to take care of it so we could play when you were back.'

'**Wait** – you've stopped playing football?' Lola asked in a quiet voice.

'Only for a little bit,' Marcus muttered, looking at the ground.

'What were you thinking?' Lola said. 'You love football, don't you?'

Marcus looked at Lola. 'I wanted to be good, and I needed someone to teach me. I needed you.'

Lola walked over to Marcus and sat cross-legged on the ground in front of him. Marcus sat opposite her, resting his back against the wall.

'I'm not the only person who can teach you how to be good at football. I mean, I'm barely good myself,' Lola said.

'But—' Marcus started. Lola didn't let him finish.

'Do you know how many good footballers there are around here who play in the Cage every day?' Lola said. 'Who do you think taught me how to play football?'

Marcus shrugged.

'It was my friends and family. We have

a whole **community** here – you have to lean on that, be a part of that.' Lola gestured around the estate.

'But that's not how it used to be. It used to just be me and you,' Marcus said.

Lola smiled. 'It used to be, and it still will be sometimes, just not all the time. When I gave you that ball and asked you to look after it, I was just trying to tell you that, even though things were changing, you'd be able to keep playing, and we'd still always be able to have a **kick around** when I was home. And that I'd always be there for you. It wasn't about *that* ball, Marcus.' She paused. 'I know how you feel, you know. I live in America now where everyone talks in funny accents, and I can't see you, your mum or any of my friends—'

'That sounds awful,' Marcus interrupted, but Lola went on.

'But there's good in that too. I got a scholarship, so I don't have to pay for uni. I've met a whole bunch of new friends, and I get to see a country that I've never been to before.' Lola sighed then locked eyes with Marcus. 'We can't get back the things we lose, not really. But we can **build new things.** That's how we grow. At least that's how I think it happens. Things change. We want them to change. We need them to change.'

'But do we?' Marcus pleaded, desperate for a different answer, not the one he knew he was going to get.

'Yes, we do,' Lola said with a grin. 'Don't try to tell me that nothing fun or interesting has happened to you since I left.'

Immediately, the Breakfast Club Investigators came to mind. His team of detectives.

Stacey, the brave leader obsessed with the supernatural.

Lise, the heart of the team, and the technology expert.

Asim, the team's brilliant artist and chief worrier.

And Marcus, he had been part of them too. He bit his lip. How had he let himself throw all that away?

'Well, maybe there's one thing that happened.' Marcus swallowed. 'But I think I messed it up.'

'Oh, really?' Lola looked at him questioningly.

'Yeah,' Marcus looked up at Lola. 'And I don't know if I can fix it.'

'Well, if there's one thing I know about friends, it's that if you're really friends with them, then you can always fix it. You just have to be willing to do the right thing.' Lola shifted round until she was sitting next to him, and *slung* an arm round his shoulders. 'The right thing?' Marcus asked. 'But what is the right thing?' 'That's for you to figure out.'

Lola pushed herself up to standing, and Marcus scrambled to his feet after her.

'Sorry about kicking your football away,' he murmured, rubbing the back of his head.

'No need to be sorry, but you're going to find it while I wait for you here – that's how we'll even that out.' Lola gave him a *gentle cuff* on the head. 'Now, go get it so we can go back to bed before your mum finds us out here and I get the telling off of a lifetime!'

Once he was back in bed, Marcus couldn't get back to sleep. His mind was reeling from his conversation with Lola. There were so many thoughts up there that he thought his head might **burst.** Marcus knew that through the mess there had to be something there, a plan, a way to fix things. He just had to figure it out . . .

Chapter Eighteen

As soon as he arrived at Breakfast Club on Monday morning, Marcus scanned the room until he found the person he was looking for.

Asim was at the end of a full table, earbuds in, painting.

Marcus took a seat across from him. He waved his hand in front of Asim's face until he took out his earbuds.

'I need your *help*,' Marcus said.

Asim looked confused. 'Didn't you get everything you needed?' he asked. 'You got the thing you lost.'

'But did *we*?' Marcus replied, giving him a knowing look. 'Did all of us?'

'Yeah, I did, actually,' Asim admitted.

'**Wait,** what? You did?' Marcus said, shocked.

'I looked around after you left. My mum's book of paintings was there, in that skip.'

'OK, well then –' Marcus tried to get back on track – 'that's great. So maybe we got the items, but did we get what we actually wanted?' Marcus's conversation with Lola was still echoing in his head. 'We can't bring back the things that we lost. Why did you want the book back?'

Asim reached down into his backpack and pulled out the notebook. It was **dirty** and a little bit wet, but still intact. He turned it round, showing both sides to Marcus.

On its front cover was a postcard of a painting, but it wasn't printed onto the card – it looked as if someone had actually painted it. The colours were *rich* and *varied.* It didn't seem to be of anything in particular, but Marcus still thought it looked cool.

Asim opened up the book and then ran his finger along the dried paint on it. His jaw tightened. 'She always had more imagination than I did. I could never paint something like this. You know, that's the reason I joined in the first place.'

'To paint.' Marcus nodded, willing Asim to speak more.

'Yeah. I thought that joining the investigators would mean that I'd see **weird** things and my imagination would grow.' Asim chuckled at the thought, then the smile faded. 'She travels a lot, my mum, and sends me postcards with little paintings on them. I started collecting them in this notebook, but then I began to think that every time she sent me a postcard she was scolding me for not having the imagination to draw like her.'

'I'm sure that's not true,' Marcus said, but Asim ignored him.

'That's why *I* threw it away, over that fence.' Asim sighed. 'But then I wanted it back because I just kept thinking that if I could see it again then maybe I'd figure something out, that maybe things would **click** in my head, and I'd be able to paint like her.'

'But you can't,' Marcus said matter-of-factly.

'No, I can't,' Asim repeated. His chin sank to his chest.

'But you can be you. No one paints like you – no one else can. You'll never be able to paint like your mum, because you have to paint like *you*.' Marcus squeezed Asim's shoulder. 'Why don't you talk to your mum?'

'I already have.' Asim's head popped back up. There was a smile on his face now.

'Wait, what?' Marcus was having a hard time keeping up.

'I said I got what I wanted, but it wasn't from this.' Asim waved the notebook in Marcus's face. 'It was from talking with my mum. I called her after I got the notebook back and we talked things through. She's in

Italy right now, doing some teaching and working on new art. She was sending me the postcards because she wanted to give me a **sneak peek** of what she's working on, but I took it so differently.' Asim shook his head.

Marcus knew the feeling; he'd taken Lola's gift of the football so completely differently from how she'd actually meant it.

'If you look at things from another angle, sometimes they can look so different,' Marcus muttered.

'Yes, yes they can.' Asim grinned. Marcus grinned back.

'You know what else we can do? We can bring the **Breakfast Club Investigators** back,' Marcus said.

'But how do we do it?' Asim asked. 'Stacey and Lise are completely out.'

Marcus frowned, the familiar feeling of **guilt** stirring in his stomach.

'It's not entirely your fault that the BCI fell apart, you know. I didn't exactly do anything to stop it,' Asim said. It was as if he could read Marcus's mind.

'Well, I have an idea,' Marcus told him. 'It's going to take some effort, but if everything goes to plan **it'll work.**'

'To plan?' Asim's eyebrows raised. 'Things don't normally go to plan with the BCI, in case you haven't noticed. Look at our plan with the chupacabra!'

'This plan is different.' Marcus waved Asim closer. 'Listen.'

Marcus laid out exactly what his plan was. And over the next couple of days they worked together. It took many hours after school, sneaking **heavy packages** of art supplies in, help from Marcus's local corner shop, Oyin and Patrick and even from Mr Anderson. And then they were finally ready.

At Breakfast Club three days later, when Stacey wasn't looking, Marcus walked over to her table and slipped a note onto it.

There were two boxes drawn on the page. **YES** was written below the one on the left. **NO** was written below the one on the right.

Marcus didn't wait around to see what her response would be. Instead he just crossed his fingers and went outside to the place he hoped she would go.

Marcus and Asim had been waiting outside the hideout for five minutes when they saw

Stacey approaching. Her mouth fell open as she took in the cabin.

'How did you fix it?' she breathed.

The hideout was *completely repaired.* A brand-new door had been installed and a whole bunch of new furniture was in the room.

'Well, we got some help,' Marcus said, grinning at her.

'Building supplies from Mr Diallo at the corner store and art supplies from the woman who runs the art store, and we got Mr Anderson and some other kids at the Breakfast Club to help us repair it,' Asim added.

Stacey frowned at him. 'Why did you do this? **It's over.**'

'Because I'm sorry for what I said. I get it now,' Marcus said.

Stacey put her hands on her hips. 'What do you get?' she asked.

'Why you're here,' Marcus cried. He glanced back at Asim. 'Why we're all here! It's because we like hanging out with each other. We like each other and being a part of BCI.

You *did* lose something Stacey, even if you said you didn't. You lost your old friends and your old community and your old life when you moved here. But it's OK, because you started the BCI, and met us, and now we're friends.' Marcus grinned.

'We *were* friends.' Stacey crossed her arms.

'No, we *are* friends.' Lise stepped out of the hideout.

'Lise?' Stacey gasped. 'I thought you said you weren't going to go back.'

'Sorry, Stace. They asked me **really, really** nicely. How was I supposed to say no?' Lise shrugged.

'But what's the point?' Stacey pressed.

'The point?' Marcus repeated.

'Yeah, why would I join again if it's all going to end in the same way?' Stacey stared off to one side and gritted her teeth. 'What if you all **leave?**' Her voice almost cracked as she said it.

'And what if that doesn't happen?' Marcus said. 'What if this works? Things can go well too.'

Stacey frowned for a moment, but she couldn't stop a grin from forming on her face.

'Well, I suppose we can't leave the mystery of the chupacabra **unsolved.** What type of detective would that make me?' Stacey ran over to the other three and hugged them.

'So, how are we going to finally finish this case?'

'Well,' Marcus said. 'I have an idea.'

Chapter Nineteen

Marcus's heart was **thumping.** Everything had been leading to this. Yet he couldn't help but wonder what would happen if they were wrong. What if this didn't work out? They were going up against a **monster:** a *chupacabra*. Or at least something that looked like a chupacabra.

'Are we ready?' Marcus glanced around at his fellow detectives.

Lise gave a confident nod.

'Probably not, but –' Asim shrugged.

'Of course!' Stacey exclaimed. 'You remember who we are?'

'We're the **Breakfast Club Investigators!**' Marcus shouted.

'The Breakfast Club Investigators!'

they all cried at once.

Marcus, Asim, Lise and Stacey were standing in the alleyway where they'd found the football, the one to which they'd tracked the chupacabra. But this time they weren't following a tracker, and they had no traps.

Marcus had been thinking about it for days. Last weekend, when they'd followed the creature, hadn't been the first time he'd gone through this alleyway. He'd been through here loads of times, just not recently. It had been with his school football team. And this wasn't just any alley – it was a *short cut.*

At the end of the alley, way past the skip, was a football ground called Stillwater Stadium.

A shout next to Marcus made him look up. **'Look!'** Stacey cried. **'It's there!'** She pointed.

Far off in the distance, they could see the chupacabra jumping over one of the side fences of the stadium.

'We need to get inside!' Marcus yelled. 'Come on!' He tried to push away his memories of what had happened the last time they'd met the chupacabra as he ran down the alleyway. Especially its **sharp teeth** and its **long claws.** It was time for them to solve this mystery.

Marcus reached the entrance to the stadium, and waited for the others to catch up. He **swallowed** hard, and nodded in determination. 'This way,' he said. He beckoned Lise, Stacey and Asim through the entrance. →

The doors of the stadium **clicked** shut behind him.

'So now we're trapped with it,' Asim murmured, not daring to raise his voice above a whisper.

'We're not locked in here with *it*. *It's* locked in here with *us*,' Stacey said in a low voice. Marcus could tell she was trying to sound much braver than she felt.

They crept into the stadium, keeping as quiet as possible, so as not to alert the creature.

At first, the space was wide and open,

but as they got deeper into the building the corridors became *more and more narrow.* Marcus exchanged nervous glances with Asim. It felt as if the entire building was *closing in* on them.

'Where is it?' Lise whispered. No one responded. 'It must be here, right?'

'It's here. *I can feel it,'* Marcus said quietly. Then he froze as the lights above flickered. The whole group stopped, **drenched** for a moment in darkness. Then the lights turned back on.

They were not alone.

The chupacabra was staring at them from the other end of the hallway.

The hair on Marcus's arms stood on edge as the chupacabra let out a long, low howl. It started to walk towards them **menacingly.**

But Marcus had a plan. With all these rooms and corridors, so many **twists** and **turns,** it would be impossible for them to trap the chupacabra by themselves. But, this time, they were not alone.

Other members of the Breakfast Club filed in behind them, standing at almost every possible turn, blocking off the chupacabra's options. Marcus saluted Oyin and Patrick as they edged behind it, making sure that it couldn't run away.

Despite his fear, Marcus grinned as he saw everyone taking their place. His plan had been to work together. With everyone here, they could actually corner the beast and get to the bottom of the **mystery.**

The chupacabra was clearly panicking with so many people surrounding it. It glanced left and right, as if looking for an escape, its shoulders raised. It let out another **blood-curdling** howl, louder this time,

and then it fixed its stare right at Marcus, Stacey, Lise and Asim.

The investigators didn't move from where they stood, in the dead centre of the corridor.

Marcus's mind was racing as he looked at the creature. The stain on Lise's hand, the oily barrel in the alleyway that had been half **spilled,** the chupacabra – Marcus knew that there was a connection between all three of these things – he just didn't know **what** it was yet. But he did have an idea of something that could help him figure it out. Patrick and Oyin had helped him set it up the day before.

This was the second part of Marcus's plan.

'Hose,' Marcus yelled suddenly. A couple of moments later a hose slithered forward, passed from person to person, until it was in Marcus's hands. He twisted its nozzle and immediately a jet of water *blasted* out, hitting the chupacabra squarely in the side. It yelped and retreated.

The entrance to the stadium was now closed, and the rest of the paths were blocked off by the other kids, so there was only one other place to which the chupacabra could run. The place they were sure it had been living.

The third changing room.

The detectives chased the chupacabra into its lair, leaving the other kids behind. They ran single file, each holding a part of the hose, and burst into the room. It was filled with an assortment of odd objects – random toys, footballs, even glasses – all the items it had been **hoarding.**

'It's all here. It's really here,' Stacey said, with wide eyes.

'Stacey — the chupacabra!' Marcus yelled.

The creature was moving so fast that it couldn't stop itself, even though it tried. It **crashed** into the wall at the back of the room. This was their chance. Marcus leaped forward and twisted the nozzle of the hose once more, letting the full force of the water come out. It collided with the creature, completely **drenching** it, and **spraying** so much water back at them that Marcus could barely see. The group yelled as cold water drenched their clothes, but they didn't retreat.

This was the moment of truth.

Dark splotches rippled away from the

chupacabra, followed by a sludgy, oily mixture. It was like the mess next to the skip. But that wasn't all. Tonnes of twigs, sticks and pieces of dead grass followed. To Marcus, it looked just like water when he had washed his muddy trainers in it. He finally turned off the hose.

The chupacabra stood up, and when it did, it looked **very different.** Instead of a dark black, its body seemed to be grey. Now that the sludgy oil was off, they could clearly see strands of wet fur *poking* out in all directions. Saliva, which looked suspiciously like the ectoplasm, was **drooling** from its mouth.

'It's a dog!' Asim cried out as it clambered forward.

It shook its body hard, spraying water all

over the room, drenching the detectives even further.

'It's a dog,' Stacey gasped. 'You were right, Marcus. It wasn't a chupacabra.' Her face **dropped.**

Marcus felt bad for her. 'I don't think so,' he said. 'Look at how big it is!'

'It's just a husky, right?' said Stacey in a small voice.

'No, I've seen big dogs before, but this is **bigger** than any dog I've ever seen.' Marcus stared at the creature, examining it from all sides. It shook itself again, **hard,** spraying even more water all over the room.

'So, what do you think it is?' Asim piped up.

Marcus paused for a moment. 'I think it's a **wolf.**'

'A wolf?' all the other detectives said at once.

'That would explain why it's so big and why it howls so much,' Marcus went on. 'And why it keeps stealing everyone's things. The wolf probably thinks this is its territory and our stuff is its stuff.'

'But there aren't any wolves where we live.' Stacey crossed her arms over her chest.

'How do you know?' Marcus replied.

'It was in the werewolf section of my book,' Stacey said. 'And why would one be just roaming around by itself?'

'Well, this is just part of a mystery that we have to solve.' Marcus grinned.

The wolf lay down and *rolled* onto its back happily, exposing its stomach.

'Nah, that's **definitely a dog,**' Lise said.

'Yep, it's very doglike,' Asim added.

'A hundred per cent dog,' Stacey said.

'*Really?!*' Marcus yelled. The four of them burst out laughing.

The dog let out a loud howl.

The other kids from the Breakfast Club

slowly began to file in. They took in the scene with wide eyes.

'Hey, my book!' someone cried.

'My glasses!' exclaimed someone else. They all went over to the masses of stuff around the room, picking out what belonged to them.

Marcus took a couple of slow steps forward, then he reached down and rubbed the dog's stomach. It **wriggled** with glee. Stacey went forward to give it a good scratch underneath its chin. The dog woofed softly.

'I think it's happy,' Lise said with a smile.

'Maybe it's pretending, before it eats us,' Asim said nervously.

'Didn't we just agree that it's a dog?' Lise replied.

'Dogs eat people too, you know,' Asim shot back.

'Asim, get over here,' Marcus called out over his shoulder.

Lise grabbed Asim's shoulders and **pushed** him towards the dog.

'Wait! Wait!' Asim tried to run away, but Lise just kept moving him forward. 'I'll come, just give me a second.' But it was too late: Asim was in front of the dog. He closed one of his eyes, and slowly reached down with a shaking hand.

The moment his hand touched its fur, it stopped shaking.

'Maybe the dog isn't that bad,' Asim said with a slowly spreading grin.

Stacey looked back at her fellow detectives. **'Case solved!'**

Stacey, Asim, Marcus and Lise whooped and cheered. The dog began to howl alongside them.

Chapter Twenty

Marcus was sitting at a table at Breakfast Club alongside his fellow detectives. They were surrounded by a huge crowd of kids, all **jostling** each other, each wanting their own case to be investigated first. They were all **shouting** so loudly that Marcus could barely make out what they were saying. Luckily, Mr Anderson was running Breakfast Club today, and he was turning a blind eye to all the commotion.

'There are **zombie squirrels** in the playground!' someone shouted.

'I'm being followed by **crows,**' a voice piped up.

'The boys' toilet is **haunted!**' someone else cried.

Stacey and Asim furiously wrote down people's requests. Marcus leaned over to Lise.

'Are we ever going to be able to get through these cases?' he said in an undertone.

'Maybe not, but having too many cases is a fun place to be,' Lise replied with a smile. 'I don't want us to **ever** run out of cases.'

'Yeah, I agree.' Marcus grinned back at her.

Marcus saw Patrick approaching their table, football in hand. 'So, what do you think, Marcus? Fancy a game after school?'

'Absolutely,' Marcus said, giving Patrick a thumbs up.

After school, Marcus was on the playground, swerving in between defenders. He turned, dodged and finally ended up in front of goal. The goalie rushed out towards him. Marcus took a shallow breath, then neatly lifted the ball over the goalkeeper and

into the *goal.*

He let out a triumphant yell as Oyin and Patrick grabbed him tight and slapped his back. Eventually, it had been them, not Lola, who'd helped him get his touch back.

'Come on, Marcus! We have a case to work,' Marcus heard Stacey call out from the sidelines.

'Sorry, guys.' He gave Oyin and Patrick a rueful smile. 'We'll finish this later. I've got to go.'

'You better!' Oyin yelled as Marcus left. 'In the meantime, **go solve that case!'**

When Marcus and Stacey burst into their new and improved hideout, the husky, which was curled up at Asim's feet, woofed happily. They'd taken the dog to the vet for a check-up after they'd left the stadium. The poor thing had been abandoned by its owner, and must have fallen into the barrel of oily gloop next to the skip at some point.

The vet had cleaned her up and said she would be taken in by the local cat and dog home. But the very next day, after badgering his parents all evening (his mum via video call), Asim had convinced them to adopt the husky. The family had called her Saint. Asim stared down at her with love in his eyes.

'So, what are we working on this time?' Marcus asked as he took a seat.

'Lise, can you turn on the projector please?' Stacey asked.

'No problem,' Lise replied, getting the machine ready.

'Are you ready?' Stacey asked the room. The detectives caught each other's eyes and grinned.

'Yeah, let's do this,' Marcus said. 'The next adventure awaits!'

The End

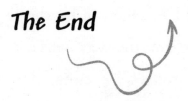

About the Authors and Illustrator

Marcus Rashford MBE

Marcus Rashford MBE is Manchester United's iconic number 10 and an England International footballer.

During the lockdown imposed due to the COVID-19 pandemic, Marcus teamed up with the food distribution charity FareShare to cover the free school meal deficit for vulnerable children across the UK, raising in excess of 20 million pounds. Marcus successfully lobbied the British Government to u-turn policy around the free food voucher programme – a campaign that has been deemed the quickest turnaround of government policy in the history of British politics – so that 1.3 million vulnerable children continued to have access to food supplies whilst schools were closed during the pandemic.

In response to Marcus's End Child Food Poverty campaign, the British Government committed £400 million to support vulnerable children across the UK, supporting 1.7 million children for the next 12 months.

In October 2020, he was appointed MBE in the Queen's Birthday Honours. Marcus has committed himself to combating child poverty in the UK and his book *You Are a Champion: How to Be the Best You Can Be* is an inspiring guide for children about reaching their full potential.

Alex Falase-Koya

Alex Falase-Koya is a London native. He has been both reading and writing since he was a teenager; anything at the cross-section of social commentary and genre fiction floats his boat. He was a winner of

Spread the Word's 2019 London Writers Awards for YA/children's. He now lives in Walthamstow with his girlfriend and two cats. He is the cowriter of Marcus Rashford's debut children's fiction title *The Breakfast Club Adventures*.

Marta Kissi

Marta Kissi studied BA Illustration & Animation at Kingston University and MA Visual Communication at the Royal College of Art. Her favourite part of being an illustrator is bringing stories to life by designing charming characters and the wonderful worlds they live in. She shares a studio with her husband James.

THE MARCUS RASHFORD BOOK CLUB

Look out for the Marcus Rashford Book Club logo – it's on books Marcus thinks you'll love!

A brilliantly illustrated, laugh-out-loud, wacky adventure through time!

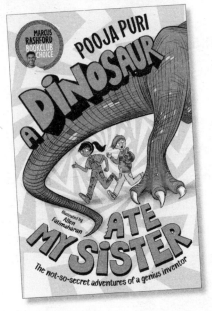

Marcus says: 'The perfect story to escape into and find adventure. Pooja is super talented and I'm a big fan!'

Marcus says: 'Fun, engaging, action-packed – I would have loved this book as a child!'

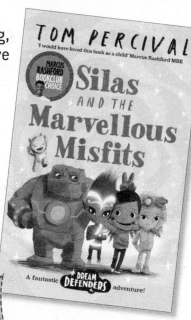

Meet the Dream Defenders! They're on a mission to banish your worries while you sleep!

Marcus says: 'Breakfast Club is about forming friendships, about togetherness, about escape. It was where some of my greatest memories were made. I want to capture that feeling in my debut fiction book'

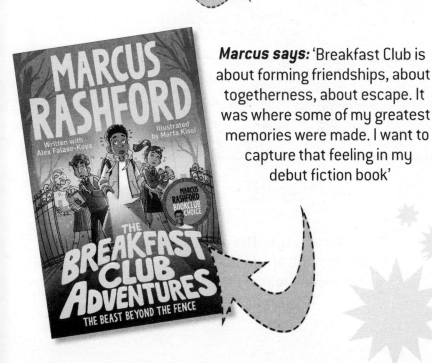

THE MARCUS RASHFORD BOOK CLUB

The Marcus Rashford Book Club is a collaboration between Marcus Rashford MBE and Macmillan Children's Books, helping children aged 8–12 to develop literacy as a life skill and a love of reading. Two books will be chosen each year by Marcus and the Macmillan team, one in summer and another in the autumn, with the mission to increase children's access to books outside of school. The book club will feature an exciting selection of titles, which aim to make every child feel supported, represented and empowered.

The book club launched in June 2021, with the fully illustrated, laugh-out-loud, time-travel adventure, *A Dinosaur Ate My Sister* by Pooja Puri, illustrated by Allen Fatimaharan, followed by *Silas and the Marvellous Misfits* by Tom Percival, an action-packed, fully-illustrated adventure that shows kids the joy of being themselves. Marcus's own book, *The Breakfast Club Adventures: The Beast Beyond the Fence*, written with Alex Falase-Koya, is the third book in the club. Copies of these books will be available in shops, and to ensure all children have access to them, free copies will also be distributed to support under-privileged and vulnerable children across the UK.

magic
breakfast
fuel for learning

You know what happens when a car runs out of fuel or battery power don't you, it just stops! Well, it's pretty much the same for people. When we don't have enough food or drink inside us, we don't have the energy we need to be able to do all the things we want and need to do in a day, like playing with friends, learning maths, or reading a favourite book. It is also really important that the food we eat is healthy, not too full of sugar, and gives us energy that will last the whole day.

Eating breakfast is particularly important as it will probably have been a long time since our last meal, so there won't be a lot of energy left in our bodies to help us learn. Magic Breakfast is a charity that works with lots of schools in England and Scotland to help them make sure all their pupils eat a healthy breakfast, so they are full of energy for the morning ahead.

Magic Breakfast is very pleased to have joined Marcus Rashford and Macmillan Children's Books to ensure thousands of schoolchildren from its partner schools receive books from Marcus Rashford's Book Club. Together we can provide breakfast to fuel learning and books to transport you to new worlds, especially for those who may have neither at home.

Magic Breakfast would also like to thank Marsh for all their support and their generous contribution to the Marcus Rashford Book Club.

 Marsh

To learn more about Magic Breakfast you can visit their website: **www.magicbreakfast.com** and remember, always have breakfast at home or at school if you can.

Being able to read, write, speak and listen well can change someone's life: these skills don't just help throughout school and work, they also support overall well-being. Books and reading are a brilliant way to boost these important literacy skills, but unfortunately the National Literacy Trust research shows that an estimated 410,000 children don't own a single book of their own. The charity is a proud partner of Marcus Rashford's Book Club to help provide children and young people with access to books and their life-changing benefits.

It's the National Literacy Trust's mission to improve the literacy levels of those who need support most. It runs Literacy Hubs and campaigns with schools and families in communities where low literacy seriously impact people's life chances. The charity has a huge range of literacy-building resources and activities online for children and young people of all ages, including complementary resources for this brilliant new Book Club.

www.literacytrust.org.uk

Hello!

Did you enjoy *The Breakfast Club Adventures*?

At KPMG we love books and the exciting new worlds they can open up to us all. That's why we're happy to support the Marcus Rashford Book Club, so that more children have access to books at school and at home.

We hope you really enjoyed your new book.

Happy reading!
From everyone at KPMG UK.

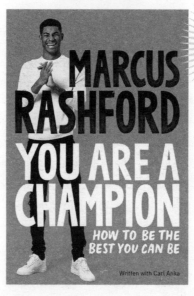

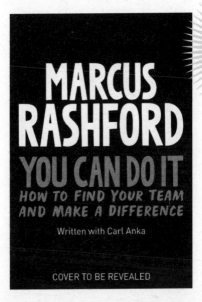

MARCUS
RASHFORD
YOU CAN DO IT
HOW TO FIND YOUR TEAM
AND MAKE A DIFFERENCE

Written with Carl Anka

COVER TO BE REVEALED

COMING
JULY
2022!

'One person isn't going to change the world, but your voice can make a huge difference.'

Marcus uses the power of his voice to shine a light on the injustices that he cares passionately about, and now he wants to help YOU find the power in yours! From surrounding yourself with the right team, to showing kindness to those around you, to celebrating and championing difference, Marcus shows you that your voice really does matter and that you can do anything you put your mind to, and that even the smallest changes can have the biggest impact.